CRUSH THE
AMERICAN
Oligarchy

CRUSH THE
AMERICAN
Oligarchy

GERALD McIsaac

Printed in the United States of America

ISBN 978-1-963068-96-2 (sc)
ISBN 978-1-963068-97-9 (hc)
ISBN 978-1-963068-95-5 (e)

Library of Congress Control Number: 2025914173

History
2025.07.03

CONTENTS

Chapter 1 Concerning Ancient Advanced Civilizations and Artifacts.....1

Chapter 2 Civil War In Syria...12

Chapter 3 Trump and the Fourteenth Amendment to the Constitution
....18

Chapter 4 Fourteenth Amendment Versus the Twelfth Amendment....32

Chapter 5 Concerning Biden's "Farewell Address To the Nation".........38

Chapter 6 Trump Once Again President 44

Chapter 7 An Open Letter To Independent Socialists 51

Chapter 8 Continuous Attacks On American Democratic Republic.....60

Chapter 9 Trump and Tariffs 68

Chapter 10 Americans Protesting Against Oligarchy...........................75

Chapter 11 American Republic Close To Collapse 82

Chapter 12 Constitutional Crisis..88

Chapter 13 Council Power 93

Chapter 14 Separate American Independent Socialist Council Republics
 99

Chapter 15 Growing Opposition to Trump and Musk 103

Chapter 16 Spiritual Power 109

Chapter 17 Celebrity Power 114

Chapter 18 Project 2025 Going Into Effect 118

Chapter 19 Concerning Allegations That Trump Is A Russian Asset.... 125

Chapter 20 Open Letter To American Workers.................................. 130

INTRODUCTION

As the title of this book suggests, it is mainly concerned with the attempt, of the American bourgeoisie, to destroy the democratic republic, and replace it with the rule of an Oligarchy. Yet it also contains articles concerning entirely different matters. For this, I make no apologies. I am concerned with matters which concern the most advanced members of the proletariat. Such workers are concerned with something more than local and even national events. But then, that is the reason they are referred to as "internationalist workers". Further, I am just as concerned with workers in other parts of the world. True internationalist workers have no country!

Aside from that, the title may not be completely accurate, but then no title is completely accurate. As long as it "passes muster". Besides, I simply cannot think of a finer title, so have decided to go with this one. Especially as my book publishers insists on a title. Who can blame them?

CHAPTER 1

Concerning Ancient Advanced Civilizations and Artifacts

It is significant that, in various countries of the world, the most advanced members of the working class, those whom Lenin refers to as "Internationalist workers", are involved in challenging scientific theories, in the field of archaeology.

In particular, they are conducting a careful examination, of the ruins of previous civilizations, especially, although not exclusively, those of the "Ancient Egyptians".

Those who investigate the ruins of "Ancient Egypt", are referred to as "Egyptologists", and include professional archaeologists, as well as amateurs. These professionals are commonly referred to as "mainstream archaeologists", while the amateurs, especially those who challenge the theories put forward by the professionals, are generally referred to in less polite terms.

As a result of these investigations, the amateur archaeologists have determined that those same "Ancient Civilizations", were far more advanced than previously thought! They almost certainly used electricity, as well as power tools! They also had the technology required to move items, such as granite statues and obelisks, which weighed tens -and even hundreds- of tons!

Further, they are convinced that, at least in Egypt, there existed a "previous civilization". Many of the statues and monuments, built by this previous civilization, was usurped by the later, "Dynastic Egyptians". They merely claimed these creations, as their own!

The fact that these "Internationalist" workers are making these bold claims, is most encouraging. It provides them with valuable training, in preparation for the forth coming revolution, and the subsequent Scientific Socialism, in the form of the Dictatorship of the Proletariat.

Most of these advanced workers, are focused on that which they refer to as "Ancient Egypt", complete with the pyramids. Properly so, I might add, as in Egypt, the evidence for an advanced civilization, which existed before the "Age of the Pharaohs", is very sharp and clear.

This calls for a little explanation, for the benefit of so many common people. First, the term BCE, Before the Common Era, has replaced BC, Before Christ.

As well, the title "Pharaoh", is that of a ruler with almost absolute power. The first Egyptian Pharaoh came to power at about 3100 BCE, at the time of the unification of the country, that of Upper and Lower Egypt. This gave rise to that which scholars refer to as the "Early Dynastic Period", in that other Dynasties followed. Those same scholars have also divided this time of rule, that of the Pharaohs, into several Periods. Yet all are agreed that the rule of the Pharaohs ended with the death by suicide, of Cleopatra, in the year 30 BCE. That also marked the beginning of Roman rule.

It is also customary to refer to the Egyptians, who lived under the rule of the Pharaoh's, as "Ancient Egyptians". May I suggest that a more accurate title is that of "Dynastic Egyptians", as those who lived before the age of Pharaohs, can also be considered to be "Ancient Egyptians".

These advanced workers have produced a great many videos, concerning the pyramids, obelisks, statues and ruins of ancient Egypt, and compared them to the ruins of other ancient civilizations, in different parts of the world. The similarities are striking.

That being said, it is also important to note that certain of these videos are of questionable significance. Even though each announcer did their best, in producing each video, there are occasions when the end result was mere confusion. For that reason, I have carefully selected, and recommend, those which I consider to be among the best.

Perhaps it would be best to start with the video titled, "Out of Place Ancient Artifacts In the Cairo Museum In Egypt".

The title of this video is somewhat misleading, as it is clear that the "Ancient Artifacts", which the announcer considers to be "Out of Place", within the "Cairo Museum", are indeed most "Ancient"! Such artifacts are most properly displayed in the Cairo Museum! Along side the "not so ancient" artifacts, which were created by the Dynastic Egyptians, so that the contrast is sharp and clear!

The video starts, within the Cairo Museum, with an examination of an "Ancient Artifact", that of a "giant, granite, unfinished box".

The narrator is correct to refer to this container as an "unfinished box", because that is precisely the case. Even though the "mainstream archaeologists" always refer to such containers as a "sarcophagus", another term for a coffin. Yet numerous such "granite boxes" have been located within Egypt, while none have been known to be used as a a coffin! Bravo, announcer!

All such "granite boxes", found within Egypt, have been carved from a single block of granite. This particular box was no exception. The only thing different, was the fact that the workmen made a mistake. The interior of the box was cut out perfectly, but the attempt to cut out a lid, from that same block of granite, resulted in a mistake, and the lid broke. This is not too surprising, as we all make mistakes. For that reason, the unfinished box was abandoned.

The narrator is also correct, when he states that it includes signs of "high technology", which includes "saw marks". In particular, there were examples of "two circular saws working, one on top, one on the bottom, obviously

     Gerald McIsaac

powered by some kind of machine, and rapidly cutting through this granite, which is seven out of ten, on the hardness scale, with diamond being ten".

For the benefit of those who do not generally work with stone, I will mention that there is something called the "Moh scale", created as a means of measuring the hardness of different minerals. As the narrator mentioned, diamond has a hardness of 10, while hardened steel has a hardness of between 7 and 8. Granite has a hardness of 6 to 7, while copper and bronze come in around 3.

Allow me to stress the fact that it is simply not possible to cut into a block of granite, with a copper or bronze tool! Those were the only tools available to the "Dynastic Egyptians"! Attempts have been made to do just that, as a means of proving that such people were capable of fashioning granite boxes! All such attempts ended in abject failure! Such tools are simply too soft! These granite boxes were not created by the Dynastic Egyptians!

The narrator went on to state that, right next to this defective granite box, is a second granite box, complete with a "different set of saw marks", possibly from a "band saw, working at high speed, and that requires a diamond encrusted blade", which "did not exist during Dynastic times, so we have to consider that these saw marks are from a much older civilization, that had high technology". Excellent!

This was followed by an examination of a "basalt box", which has a hardness of about 6. It too, was clearly made with "advanced technology", by an earlier civilization, then "recycled" by the Dynastic Egyptians, who were able to claim it as their own.

The narrator then proceeded to the second floor of the museum, and was struck by the fact that there were two sarcophagi, each "ten foot long", or three meters. He was skeptical that people grew that large!

Such an attitude is understandable, but perhaps mistaken. As I have documented in previous articles, we are not the only species of human, currently living on this planet! The humans known as "gigantopithecus", is also very much alive and well. They grow to a height of "ten feet", or three meters. I refer to them as "Giants". It is entirely possible that the mummified remains of these Giants is located within these sarcophagi. A simple DNA test would prove this, or disprove it. It is worth a shot, but not likely to happen. No doubt the mainstream scientists are dead set opposed to this. Perish forbid that I should be proven correct!

The next item on the "hit parade", is the "Enigmatic Schist Disk", so called because it appears to be made out of the mineral schist. Or not. No one seems to know the possible use of such a disk. Yet as it was found in an ancient tomb, it must have been held in high regard. After all, only such items were buried with the dead.

Without doubt, it was meant to "rotate and resonate", to "vibrate". As it was found in pieces, and put back together as best the workers could, the original shape could have been slightly different.

It is entirely possible that it was used in the process of "melting stones", and forming different blocks. More on that subject later, in this article.

This disk was found in a "cache of thirty thousand to forty thousand turned, very hard stone bowls and plates, that could only have been made, using lathes of some kind". It is significant that many of these containers were made of granite!

Even the labels on these objects, states that they were likely from the "Pre Dynastic or Archaic Period".

The narrator is correct, when he states that these artifacts, including granite bowls, could have been created only on a machine powered lathe. Yet he neglected to mention that such a machine had to be powered by electricity!

This is followed by a display of hand crafted pottery, created during the Dynastic Period. The contrast is striking! The quality of workmanship is far inferior!

The narrator concluded that there was an earlier civilization, which existed possibly twelve thousand years ago, and was far superior to the Dynastic Egyptians. Not something the mainstream archaeologists want to hear!

This begs the question: What was the power source for these machines?

The answer to this question was revealed, in the excellent video, "Pyramids Power Plant Theory - Proof and Experiments". The "Great Pyramid of Gaza", one of the "Seven Wonders of the Ancient World", was nothing other than an electrical generator! It used the Nile River to produce vast amounts of electricity!

The narrator also documented the fact that the "Granite Sarcophagi" were also nothing other than giant batteries!

The electrical power from these sources, was used to illuminate the underground labyrinths, to provide power to run lathes, as well as huge stone cutters.

Truly, the idea that the pyramids were "constructed as tombs", is "completely ridiculous"! They were electrical generators! We can learn from the "Archaic Egyptians"!

This brings us to a subject I merely touched upon, earlier in the article, that of "melting stones". That is covered in another video, that of "Mystery of Ancient 'Knobs' In Temples - Evidence of Stone Melting - Geopolymer Technology?"

The video is set in Cambodia and India. The narrator points out that, on the walls of stone temples, certain stone blocks have a mysterious protrusion, called "knobs", a "projection like a door knob". Most stone blocks do not have these protrusions. Yet he pointed out that the stones which have such "protrusions", also have plants growing out of them!

As he stated, in reference to the walls of the temples, "This is all solid granite, huge blocks perfectly fit together, you cannot even insert a needle between these blocks, they look as though they are molded and assembled." He further concluded that the stones with knobs were "defective pieces from a mass manufacturing company"! They are "not only found in Cambodia and India, but also in Egypt, Peru, Turkey and almost all ancient megalithic sites".

He went on to explain that these "knobs" are called "drops" in the field of casting. As he stated, "When we melt some material and pour it into a die, sometimes if the material has not fully liquified, it forms a projection, technically known as 'Drops'…. The ancients were melting and casting rocks, just as we form concrete blocks today. …Rocks were melted and some other ingredient was added. Plants grow only on stone blocks of ancient temples, probably because the rocks are softer than natural rocks….. Rocks melted, material added, into geo polymers…. Melting rocks a well known concept in Hinduism. Such priests say they were created artificially, man made stones, possible herbs which can soften or liquify stone. This allows for rock bending technology".

Assuming that these huge rocks were "melted and casted", as I suspect is the case, then without doubt, something was added to these rocks, in order to make them soft and malleable. Perhaps the best way to determine the exact chemical additive, is to take a sample of a block, one with plants growing out of it, and subject it to a proper analysis, in a laboratory.

There are other mysteries, although not quite so ancient. These are covered quite well in the video, "10 Unsolved Mysteries of Ancient Rome".

One of these "Unsolved Mysteries" is that which is referred to as the "Roman Dodecahedron", a "geometrical shape with twelve faces". It also has "tiny knobs on each outer edge", and "holes of various sizes on each face". Over one hundred of these "peculiar objects" have been found, all over Europe. Yet "no one has any idea what they were used for", as there is "no mention of such an item in any historical record". This has not stopped people from putting forward various suggestions, such as "candle holders", to "mere decorations".

As the Romans were both practical and not at all sentimental, these suggestions are not likely. I consider it far more likely that these were mere toys, used for gambling. This would explain the fact that they are not mentioned in the historical record.

As is well known, all armies are plagued with the problem of boredom. This was especially true before the invention of the printing press, which helped to alleviate the problem, through the written word. Of course, the Romans had no access to this. Partly for that reason, they tended to relieve boredom with gambling, frequently with the use of dice.

The thieves of the time were not stupid. They noticed that dice were small, easily concealed and switched, with dice that were "loaded". That is true to this day.

It is very likely that the "dodecahedron" was invented, as an alternative to a pair of dice. Much larger, not so easily concealed and switched, and with holes on each face, so that it was not so easy to "load them". Possibly each face was numbered, in chalk, from 1 to 12, or in Roman numerals, from I to XII. Or perhaps these numbers were scratched into each face. If that is the case, then a few of those items should still have these marks on them.

I mention this as an example of facing these "Ancient Mysteries", on an individual basis. This is referred to as "Eating the apple one bite at a time". This makes more sense than trying to solve all such mysteries at once.

Now to return to our investigation of Ancient Egyptian Technology.

One of the finest videos is titled, "The Pyramid, the Labyrinth, and the Underground Caches of Hawara". It documents the difficulties that these "amateur archaeologists" are facing, as they challenge "mainstream accepted" scientific theories, in the field of archaeology.

The video starts with a quote by an ancient Greek writer, by the name of Herodacus, the "Father of Historians". As he stated, writing around 500 BCE:

"This I have actually seen. A work beyond words. For if anyone put together the building of the Greeks, and display of their labours, they would seem lesser, in both efforts and expense, to this Labyrinth. Even the pyramids are beyond words. Yet the Labyrinth surpasses even the pyramids."

Coming from a highly respected Greek historian, this is indeed "high praise"!

He went on to describe a "multi level structure called Labyrinth", one which contained "three thousand rooms filled with hieroglyphs and paintings". Half of these rooms were underground!

Other ancient travellers support this description, at least of the above ground structures. These include such highly respected sources as Strabo and Pliny.

If true, then this structure would qualify as the "Eighth Wonder of the Ancient World"! Yet no trace of this Labyrinth has ever been found. Or at least, not until now!

Modern day amateur archaeologists are convinced that the above ground structure has been destroyed and "scavenged", the material used by successive generations, in order to construct new buildings. They are also convinced that the underground structures are still intact!

In 2008, a professional team of geo physicists, equipped with ground penetrating radar, conducted a survey, in that area. As a result of that survey, they concluded that there is a strong possibility that the Labyrinth may still exist. Their results were published in the "National Research Institute of Astronomy and Geophysics", under the title of "Geophysical Studies of Hawara Pyramid Area".

This could well have led to a major scientific breakthrough. The existence of the Labyrinth could have been proven! The Egyptian authorities were quick to "express their appreciation", so to speak. In fact, the Supreme Council of Antiquities ordered them to "stop communicating" those results, or face "sanctions", from the "Egyptian National Security". Gratitude!

This unfortunate response, to scientific research which challenges mainstream scientific theories, is not exceptional. It is typical. Also reactionary! All too many leaders, of all too many countries, are determined to "Maintain the status quo", to make sure that "Nothing changes", that everything "Stays precisely the way it is". "The text books have been written, and they are to stay written, as is"!

This is not to say that the leaders of these countries are completely reactionary. In scientific jargon, we say that these leaders, who oppose such challenges, "have certain reactionary features".

As I have documented in previous writings, this is precisely the attitude which has led to the collapse of numerous previous civilizations. Not that it is about to lead to the collapse of our civilization, as our civilization is the one and only civilization, to have experienced an industrial revolution.

That industrial revolution gave birth to two new, revolutionary classes. On the one hand, there was the capitalist class, the bourgeois. On the other hand, as no class can exist in isolation, there was also the working class, the proletariat.

Yet that changed dramatically, at around the beginning of the twentieth century. At that time, capitalism reached the stage of monopoly. The age of revolutionary competitive capitalism was over. The age of reactionary monopoly capitalism began. That is our current situation.

At the same time, the working class, the proletariat, has become ever more revolutionary.

It was Marx who conducted a scientific examination of capitalism, and proved that it would, of necessity, lead to a state of Scientific Socialism, in the form of the Dictatorship of the Proletariat. That is the reason our civilization will not collapse, as have all previous civilizations.

With that in mind, may I suggest that members of the revolutionary working class, the proletariat, take part in the formation of a broad based, Archaeological Society. May I further recommend that it be International, open to amateur as well as professionals, both scholars and scientists. There is strength in numbers!

The Egyptian Supreme Council of Antiquities may be able to threaten individuals with "sanctions", but not a whole Society! The country relies heavily on tourism! Such a threat would damage the tourist industry!

The preceding was a mere sample of the "Mainstream Archaeological" theories, being challenged by working people. These people deserve our support. After all, we can learn a great deal from the "Ancients".

Allow me to stress the fact that the most important thing, is the training these workers are receiving, in the class struggle. And it most definitely is a class struggle! After all, the governments of all capitalist countries, are in the service of the capitalists.

This training will serve them well, at the time of the insurrection, as well as after the revolution, when they are placed in positions of authority. Bear in mind that the most advanced workers will be placed in such positions.

As the monopoly capitalists, the bourgeoisie, are determined to strengthen their rule, thus further impoverishing the working class, the proletariat, it is clear that the working class may soon have no choice but to rise up in insurrection.

Scientific Socialism, in the form of the Dictatorship of the Proletariat, may indeed be closer than we had anticipated.

CHAPTER 2

Civil War In Syria

For fifty three years, the Assad family has ruled Syria, with an "iron hand". Absolutely no dissent was allowed. Yet on December 8, 2024, the Assad rule came to an "abrupt end". This after a mere one week rebellion!

It is no exaggeration to say that the "world is in shock". The mainstream journalists are completely amazed! To think that such a revolution could be so successful, so quickly!

Clearly, those same journalists have no idea of the power of a "popular uprising". Or at the very least, they pretend to be unaware!

This is not too surprising, as all mainstream journalists are in the service of the monopoly capitalists, the multi billionaires, the bourgeoisie. For that reason, it is in their best interest to promote that which best serves their "Lords and Masters".

They are careful to avoid any mention of the word "revolution"! Those taking part in this revolution, are being referred to as "rebels". They are not rebels! They are revolutionaries! They are fighting for national liberation! What is more, they are succeeding!

These revolutionaries consist of a broad assortment of people, from different ethnic groups, minorities and religions. In the interest of the revolution, they have agreed to put aside their differences and unite, with the goal of overthrowing the hated Assad regime.

It is significant that a major mainstream news outlet, sat down "for an exclusive interview", with the "main rebel leader, Abu Muhammad Al Valani".

The person conducting the interview, asked a good question: "In a matter of days, you have managed to take large cities. What has changed? How were you able to do this now?"

According to the translator, the reply was: "In recent years, there has been a *unification of internal opinions,* and the establishment of institutional structures, within the liberated areas of Syria. This institutionalization included the restructuring within military factions. They entered *unified training camps,* and developed a *sense of discipline.* This *discipline* allowed them ….to engage in a battle in *an organized manner.* The progress and execution of plans have been swift, with *clear communication* and *adherence to commands.* They stop where they should stop, and withdraw where they should withdraw. The *revolution* has transitioned from *chaos and randomness,* to a *state of order,* both in civil and institutional matters, and in military operations alike." (My italics)

I have chosen to include his complete response, as it is so important. The key details I have placed in italics.

The *"unification of internal opinions",* is a reference to the fact that a successful revolution, "cannot be made by an individual", so to speak. It must have "broad based support". The vast majority of common people, workers, farmers and small business owners, must be prepared to set aside their differences, and unite in the common cause, that of overthrowing the existing state apparatus.

He also mentioned *"unified training camps",* in which those same revolutionaries developed a *"sense of discipline,* which enabled them to engage in battle in an *organized manner".*

Anyone who doubts the importance of discipline, is free to consider the results of the numerous incidents, through out history, of a group of farmers, armed with pitch forks, attacking a well disciplined army of soldiers. All such outcomes, while predictable, were never pretty. The farmers were cut to pieces.

This brings us to *"clear communication and adherence to command"*. The leaders of the revolution must be well respected. Their orders must be "sharp and clear". In response, all "enlisted personnel" must be prepared to obey those orders, even if they do not agree with them. These orders may include that of "withdraw".

It is in this way, and only in this way, that the *"revolution"* can transition from *"chaos and randomness, to a state of order"*.

This brings me to a passage, written by Lenin, in Left Wing Communism, An Infantile Disorder. It is supremely relevant:

"The fundamental law of revolution, which has been confirmed by all revolutions, and especially by all three Russian revolutions in the twentieth century, is as follows: for a revolution to take place, it is not enough for the exploited and oppressed masses to realize the impossibility of living in the old way, and demand changes; for a revolution to take place, it is essential that the exploiters should not be able to live and rule in the old way. It is only when the *"lower classes" do not want* to live in the old way, and the "upper classes" *cannot carry on in the old way,* that the revolution can triumph. This truth can be expressed in other words: revolution is impossible without a nation wide crisis (affecting both the exploited and the exploiters). It follows that, for a revolution to take place, it is essential, first, that a majority of the workers (or at least a majority of the class conscious, thinking and politically active workers) should realize that revolution is necessary, and that they should be prepared to die for it; second, that the ruling classes should be going through a governmental crisis, which draws even the most backward masses into politics (symptomatic of every genuine revolution is a rapid, tenfold and even hundred fold increase in the size of the working and oppressed masses - hitherto apathetic - who are capable of waging the political struggle), weakens the government, and makes it possible for the revolutionaries to rapidly overthrow it." (italics by Lenin)

The current situation in Syria, certainly fits the "fundamental law of revolution"! The "exploited and oppressed masses", the common people, the workers and family farmers, can "no longer live in the old way", and are "demanding change". At the same time, the "exploiters", in this case the Assad regime, can no longer "rule in the old way". Revolutionary!

Syria is in a position where it has been crushed and exploited by the Assad family, for many years. At the same time, the competing imperialist powers are anxious to "exert their influence" over the country.

As Lenin explained quite well, in Imperialism, the Highest Stage of Capitalism, the whole world has long since been divided up, between the so called "Great Powers", which is to say the imperialist powers. As he phrased it, "The characteristic feature of this period is the final partition of the globe - not in the sense that a *new partition* is impossible - on the contrary, new partitions are inevitable - but in the sense that the colonial policy of the capitalist countries has *completed* the seizure of the unoccupied territories on our planet". (italics by Lenin)

The two great imperialist powers, the United States and Russia, are fighting over Syria, as two dogs fight over a bone. Both are determined to crush and exploit the country, preferably with the help of neighbouring countries.

The current situation in Syria can perhaps best be compared to the situation in Russia, immediately after the Great October Socialist Revolution of 1917. At that time, the country was in ruins, after three years of war. The infrastructure of the country was badly damaged. The common people were calling for "peace, land and bread". Many of the factories were shut down. The trains were barely running, if at all. The Russian army was in no position to fight. The situation was desperate, and desperate times call for desperate measures.

Lenin responded to this seemingly hopeless situation, by enacting a series of compromises. He persuaded the Russian Communist Party to sign the Treaty of Brest Litovsk. Even though it meant losing a third of the population, half of their industry, and ninety percent of their coal mines, as well as having to pay a huge sum in "indemnities", it was better than complete defeat.

He also made certain concessions to other political parties, within the new government. Bear in mind that none of these concessions violated principle.

As a result of these compromises, the Russian Soviet Republic was able to weather the following three year civil war, as numerous foreign powers tried to wipe out the upstart Socialist republic.

Of course, the current situation in Syria is not that desperate. Yet it is safe to say that the country has been severely damaged, after fifty years of Assad rule. No doubt, the infrastructure needs repair, various factories have been shut down, and countless people are in desperate need of the basic necessities of life, such as food, shelter and medical assistance.

As well, according to the internet, over five million Syrians have fled to neighbouring countries. They are currently living in shelters, composed of tents. It is only proper to bring them home, to rebuild their houses, to offer them at least the basic necessities, so that they can live a life of dignity.

That is going to take a certain amount of time and effort. Yet the result will be a new, improved, strong Syria, so that it is well worth it.

In the mean time, may I suggest tolerating the presence of Russian and American military bases, within Syria, as well as the Israeli occupation of the Golan Heights.

Even though the Syrian army was able to overthrow the Assad regime, very quickly, it is as yet, too weak to challenge the military power of those countries.

This may be a "bitter pill to swallow", but makes more sense than fighting a battle that cannot be won. At least, not yet! After the country is rebuilt, the infrastructure repaired, the refugees returned, factories working, trains running, farmers growing their crops, and the new Syrian Army is properly trained and equipped, then it will be a different matter.

That was precisely the policy of the newly created Russian Soviet Republic, immediately after their revolution. It served them supremely well, at least until the capitalists were able to return to power, after the death of Stalin.

The current situation in Syria is not as desperate, as was that of Soviet Russia, immediately after their revolution. Yet as the Russian Soviets were able to recover, so too, the revolutionary Syrians can also recover. As long as they do not "bite off more than they can chew".

Now is the time to consolidate. May I suggest a slogan of "Return, Repair, Rebuild". The refugees can be encouraged to return, to help repair and rebuild the country of Syria. I am sure that the vast majority are quite anxious to do just that! That is the policy which provides the Syrian Revolution, with the best chance of continued success.

CHAPTER 3

Trump and the Fourteenth Amendment to the Constitution

As I write this, Donald Trump is, once again, the "President Elect", as he, once again, won the "Presidential Election" of November, 2024, just as he did in 2016. For that reason, he is, once again, preparing to take the oath of office, just as he did, eight years ago. Except that this time, Donald Trump is well prepared.

As I have previously documented the fact that such a "Presidential Election" is completely fraudulent, in direct violation of the Twelfth Amendment to the Constitution, there is no need to go into it here.

It is also a fact that, once again, there is strong opposition to the fact that Donald Trump is about to be sworn into office, as the President of the United States, just as there was, eight years ago. Except that this time, the opposition is also much better prepared.

In 2017, the opposition came mainly from the "Women's Movement", as most of the protesters were women. Now, in 2025, the opposition appears to be far more broad based, and for that reason, far stronger.

In support of that statement, may I refer the skeptical reader to an excellent video, on the internet, produced by American Voices Unfiltered, Episode 412.

It is titled, 14th Amendment, Trump Barred, Thousands March to Stop Trump Presidency!, Will Congress Use 14th Amendment? The narrators are identified as "Ethan and Ola".

It is clear that these two individuals are well educated, well spoken, professional members of the middle class. They are certainly not Marxists, or even Leftist people. They are deeply concerned with the democratic republic, and the threat Trump poses to that republic. I consider those two to be among the finest of the bourgeois journalists.

They have produced a video which is, at least superficially, a thoughtful, balanced presentation, in that they state the details of the opposition to the swearing in of Trump, as the President, as well as the possible consequences of those actions. Yet as they cannot think in terms of class, they frequently resort to flights of fantasy and conjecture. This is characteristic of middle class intellectuals.

On the one hand, they state the facts, quite accurately. On the other hand, as they are not Scientific Socialists, Marxists, or even Leftist people, they are unable to think in terms of class struggle, which include revolution. Yet they describe the preparations for that revolution!

It is also significant that they avoid any use of profanity, of any vulgarity. The same cannot be said, of all too many Leftist writers. Perhaps those Leftist people think that the use of such vulgarity serves to emphasize the point they are trying to make. It does not. It is a mere display of ignorance, disrespectful of the reader. There can be no excuse for this behaviour.

Now to the substance of the video, which I have tried to copy, as accurately as possible, even though it is disjointed, and includes numerous grammatical errors:

"Protests erupt demanding Congress to bar Trump from office using the 14th Amendment

"Things are getting a little messy, which might be putting it lightly. There is a whole movement gaining steam, to stop the Inauguration. They are using some legal arguments, focusing of the 14th Amendment, barring anyone who has been involved in an Insurrection, from holding office. We are talking Section 3."

This calls for a little explanation. With the end of the Civil War, in 1865, and the subsequent abolition of slavery, the newly emancipated slaves became American citizens, but were frequently denied their democratic rights. In response to this, it is to the credit of the American government, that they passed the Fourteenth Amendment to the Constitution, in 1868. It is Section 3, of the Fourteenth Amendment, that the protesters are using, in an attempt to keep Trump from taking the oath of office. For that reason, I have chosen to copy that Section:

"Section 3

"No person shall be a Senator or Representative in Congress, or elector of President and Vice-President, or hold any office, civil or military, under the United States, or under any State, who, having previously taken an oath, as a member of Congress, or as an officer of the United States, or as a member of any State legislature, or as an executive or judicial officer of any State, to support the Constitution of the United States, shall have engaged in insurrection or rebellion against the same, or given aid or comfort to the enemies thereof. But Congress may by a vote of two-thirds of each House, remove such disability."

Now to proceed with the substance of the video. The narrators are referring to the "Events of January 6, 2021", which has been referred to as an "Insurrection", within the capitol of Washington, D.C., as well as the role played by Trump:

"People are really fired up over this. The big question, the heart of this whole thing, is what happened on January 6, actually meets that definition? Legally speaking, does it qualify as an Insurrection? The million dollar question! Some legal experts say yes. Trumps actions leading up to January 6, the findings from the January 6 Committee. There is already a court ruling from Colorado, that says that Trump did engage in Insurrection, so there is precedent. This sounds pretty open and shut. Trump was involved, there is a legal basis for it. End of story."

Well spoken! If only it was that simple! Yet it is not that simple, as we live in a class society, under capitalism. For that reason, no branch of the government is completely "impartial". On the contrary, all branches serve the same class of monopoly capitalists, the multi billionaires, the bourgeoisie. Yet as the narrators are careful to make no mention of classes, it is clear that they are either not aware of this, or are simply incapable, of understanding the fact that classes exist, as well as the struggle between the classes.

The narrators proceed to state:

"But then the Supreme Court kind of muddied the waters. They are saying that it is the job of Congress to enforce this part of the 14th Amendment, which is where things get really interesting. To block Trump certification, you will need a fifth of Congress to object, and then a majority to actually agree to sustain that objection, and right now, Republicans have that slim majority in both the House and the Senate. Could enough of them turn against Trump? It is a long shot, to put it mildly."

As Congress, which is to say the House of Representatives, has 435 Members, this means that eighty seven Members, which is a fifth of them, would have to "object", in order to "block Trump certification". As well, a "majority", or 218 Members, would have to "agree to sustain that objection". All according to the Supreme Court! This is commonly referred to as "passing the buck"!

Yet to refer to this as a "long shot", is not entirely accurate. In fact, it largely depends upon the strength of the revolutionary motion. As the "popular uprising" is now very powerful, and further, as each Member of Congress serves a mere two year term, it is reasonable to expect a considerable number of them to become "sweetly reasonable", when faced with the threat of being voted out of office, during the next election. The power of revolution!

It is no exaggeration to say that the current situation is completely revolutionary! In fact, a full scale revolution could break out, at any time! This is based upon an article which Lenin wrote, titled Left Wing Communism, An Infantile Disorder. I recommend that article, to all readers. Especially relevant is the following paragraph:

"The fundamental law of revolution, which has been confirmed by all revolutions, and especially by all three Russian revolutions in the twentieth century, is as follows: for a revolution to take place, it is not enough for the exploited and oppressed masses to realize the impossibility of living in the old way, and demand changes; for a revolution to take place, it is essential that the exploiters should not be able to live and rule in the old way. It is only when the *'lower classes' do not want* to live in the old way, and the 'upper classes' *cannot carry on in the old way,* that the revolution can triumph. This truth can be expressed in other words: revolution is impossible without a nation wide crisis (affecting both the exploited and the exploiters). It follows that, for a revolution to take place, it is essential, first, that a majority of the workers (or at least a majority of the class conscious, thinking, and politically active workers), should fully realize that revolution is necessary, and that they should be prepared to die for it; second, that the ruling classes should be going through a governmental crisis, which draws even the most backward masses into politics (symptomatic of any genuine revolution is a rapid, tenfold and even hundredfold increase in the size of the working and oppressed masses- hitherto apathetic- who are capable of waging the political struggle), weakens the government, and makes it possible for the revolutionaries to rapidly overthrow it." (italics by Lenin)

The significance of this particular video, lies in the fact that these two middle class narrators, document the fact that the situation is completely revolutionary! Without realizing this, of course!

Now to proceed with our video:

"It is like we are watching a political thriller unfold, but it is real life, happening right now, and to make things even more intense, there is this protest, planned in DC, this weekend, leading up to the certification vote. Expect disruption from MAGA, both sides bracing themselves for a showdown, a fundamental clash, between those who see the 14th Amendment against Trump taking office, and those who see this as a straight up attempt to overturn a democratic election. Both sides are really passionate about their views. People deeply divided, you have people completely convinced that this is the only way to stop Trump, and they are not holding back, they are ready to fight for it."

For the benefit of those who are not aware, the term "MAGA", stands for Make America Great Again, the slogan of Trump's election campaign.

Once again, the narrators have "hit the nail right on the head"! It is indeed a "political thriller", truly "happening right now", in "real life", "both sides" are "passionate", preparing for a "showdown", a "fundamental clash"! The country is indeed "deeply divided", with the protesters "not holding back"! That is the very definition of a full scale revolution! Class warfare!

The narrators proceed to state:

"But there are others who are not so optimistic, they say peaceful protest has not worked before, and that the time to act was back on election day. It is like they have lost faith in the system."

This is excellent! They just documented the fact that so many common people, by whom I mean workers and family farmers, are now somewhat more class conscious! At least to the extent that they are aware that "peaceful protest has *not* worked before", and will very likely *not* work again! They have "lost faith in the system". It stands to reason that they are now aware that "half measures get us nowhere"! Or at the very least, they are "moving in that direction"! It is the "system", which is to say the *state apparatus,* which has to be *destroyed! Smashed!*

Now to proceed with the video:

"The other question is, what if Trump is disqualified? What happens then? Hypothetically. Harris could become president. All kinds of scenarios are being thrown out, including Vance becoming President, taking over, that would change things. Highlights the uncertainty, the possibility for even more political chaos, regardless of the outcome."

Most unfortunate. Up until this point, the narrators were doing very well, stating the facts and pointing out the implications. But with this "hypothetical" scenario, they lost their way. Completely pointless. On the other hand, they managed to quickly recover, if only temporarily:

"This whole situation is completely unprecedented. There is no roadmap for this. The consequences will be huge, at a turning point in American history."

With this statement, they managed to get back on track. True, the "consequences will be huge", as we have indeed reached a "turning point in American history". Yet it is incorrect to say that "this whole situation is completely unprecedented". In fact, there is indeed a "roadmap for this". That "roadmap" was provided by the First American Revolution, of 1776.

The Declaration of Independence provides the "roadmap". As it clearly states,

"The unanimous Declaration of the thirteen united States of America, When in the Course of human events, it becomes necessary for one people to dissolve the political bands which have connected them with another, and to assume among the powers of the earth, the separate and equal station to which the Laws of Nature and of Nature's God entitle them, a decent respect to the opinions of mankind requires that they should declare the causes which impel them to the separation.

"We hold these truths to be self-evident, that all men are created equal, that they are endowed by their Creator with certain unalienable Rights, that among these are Life, Liberty and the pursuit of Happiness.--That to secure these rights, Governments are instituted among Men, deriving their just powers from the consent of the governed, --That whenever any Form of Government becomes destructive of these ends, it is the Right of the People to alter or to abolish it, and to institute new Government...."

Americans! Behold your "roadmap"! Your "Founding Fathers" have blessed you with the right to "alter or abolish", any government which does not "derive their just powers from the consent of the governed"! As your current government does not have your consent, then you have the *right to abolish* that government! We can even go so far as to say that it is your *duty to abolish* that government!

You are indeed blessed! You are perhaps the only people who have that right! Use it or lose it! Do not squander it! Exercise your democratic right to abolish the government, which does not represent you! You have done it before, you can do it again! Follow in the footsteps of your revolutionary ancestors!

Now to return to the video, and the point where the narrators reveal their middle class background:

"All because of the Fourteenth Amendment. And how did something written 150 years ago, become part of this massive political showdown? The Amendment has changed over time, originally set up to protect the rights of freed slaves, which was very important, but over time, its meaning has expanded. Living, breathing document that keeps adapting. The stakes could not be higher. We are talking about the peaceful transfer of power, which is the foundation of American democracy. Also ethical and legal questions, about whether Trump is even fit to hold office. This collision of our most basic values, and the questions that this bring up, go way beyond Trump himself. How are we as a society, going to deal with these kinds of issues in the future, because these are tough questions, are we willing to uphold the Constitution, even when it is hard?"

The preceding is nothing other than middle class whining. To blame a Constitutional Amendment, for their current predicament, is completely ridiculous. It is not even clear whether they are whining because people are trying to stop Trump from being sworn in, or because the "Constitution is a living, breathing document that keeps adapting". It is clear that they consider the "peaceful transfer of power", to be the "foundation of our American democracy". This despite the fact that the United States was borne out of violent revolution! A complete muddle.

After this flight of fantasy, they managed to get back on track, once again, if only temporarily:

"How much power should the people, should activism actually have? Questions with no easy answers. Not an abstract legal battle, it is real, it is effecting peoples lives, right now, their voices need to be heard".

The question is legitimate, and the answer is simple. The "people", those who are workers and family farmers, should have *all* the power. That is a fact. It is also a fact that, as we currently live under capitalism, it is the monopoly capitalists, those with tens and hundreds of billions, the bourgeoisie, who are in charge. Those same multi billionaires are also determined that the "people", the workers and farmers, should have no power, whatsoever.

These middle class narrators seem to be incapable of grasping the fact that we live in a class society. They appear to be searching for a "happy medium", in which power is shared between the classes. No chance! The one and only alternative to the rule of the monopoly capitalists, the multi billionaires, is Scientific Socialism, in the form of the Dictatorship of the Proletariat. Yet the narrators tried their best to "keep up their spirits", as they pointed out the obvious:

"One comment stuck with me, a feeling of impending doom, no matter what happens. Worried that if Trump is disqualified, his supporters are going to become even more distrustful of the government, even more disillusioned".

Imagine that! Could it be that this "feeling of impending doom", is the result of high inflation, massive unemployment, homelessness, drug and alcohol addiction, overdoses, frequent mass shootings, gang violence, lawlessness and the widespread corruption within the government? Are such people even capable of becoming more disillusioned? More distrustful of the government?

The narrators went on to point out the obvious:

"But if he is allowed to take office, it will legitimize what happened on Jan 6, and it sets a dangerous precedent, loss for them, a real sense of hopelessness, a lot of despair".

These people seem torn, between allowing Trump to be sworn in as President, and stopping him, using the Constitution. "Damned if you do, and damned if you do not"! Feel free to make up your mind!

They then resort to a trace of optimism:

"But others are clinging to this hope, that this whole challenge to the 14th could be a turning point, a chance to reaffirm our commitment to these democratic values. Has exposed this raw nerve in the American psyche, civic engagement has become so important, even when the outcome is so uncertain".

We cannot help but wonder, just what "turning point" they have in mind? Certainly not revolution and the subsequent Scientific Socialism, in the form of the Dictatorship of the Proletariat, as they are simply incapable of imagining such an event! Yet that is precisely the case!

This is followed by some valuable facts:

"Fourteen Now Organizers are now getting ready for these protests, coordinating transportation, have legal observers lined up, even offering training in non violent resistance techniques. Creating a space where people can exercise their First Amendment rights to free speech, while limiting the risk of violence. Not a top down movement, not being run by some big political machine, a coalition of grass roots groups, different people, different experiences, coming together, organic. Everyday people joining forces, believe in this, believe this is a fight worth having".

Now that is good to know! Such a broad based coalition is an indication of a very strong revolution!

The narrators then revert to pessimism:

"But then there is a whole debate if this whole Fourteenth Amendment strategy is the right move. Not everyone is on board. Could backfire, make things worse, could be seen as a partisan power grab, which would merely further inflame tensions, fuel the conspiracy theories that are already out there. A valid concern, already volatile situation, and even if this whole movement succeeds, it is not going to magically fix something. Will not erase these deep divisions in our society. It is not going to make everyone trust our institutions again, or bring everyone together, although that would be nice".

Of course, "Not everyone is on board"! That is because we live in a class society! Those who oppose this "popular uprising", this revolutionary motion, are the same people who serve the monopoly capitalist class! Belly crawling boot lickers, one and all! There is no shortage of such vermin!

The narrators then resort to a stab at philosophy:

"This situation, no matter what happens, is just the beginning, the start of a much bigger conversation, about accountability, the rule of law, the very foundation of our democracy. We have to look in the mirror, and ask some really tough questions, about who we are as a nation, what are our values, to tolerate, what kind of future are we trying to build. And this is not just happening in DC, also happening online, in living rooms all over the country. People are trying to make sense of it all. Trying to figure out where I stand, what is my role in all of this".

Are these people on drugs? They accurately described a revolutionary situation, and "this is just the beginning". True! But not the beginning of a "much bigger conversation"! Give your "head a shake"! It is the beginning of a revolution! Not a conversation! Indeed, "people are trying to make sense of it all"! They will soon come to realize that the "future" is in Scientific Socialism, in the form of the Dictatorship of the Proletariat! Wake up!

After that further diversion into fantasy, the narrators "return to earth", with the following statement:

"Legal experts think that this whole Fourteenth argument could end up in front of the Supreme Court. If that happens, the entire country will be glued to their screens, a landmark case".

Now they are talking! That is our most fervent hope! It is in this manner that the level of awareness of the common people, the workers and family farmers, will be raised. From their own bitter experience, they will learn that Marx and Lenin were correct, that the monopoly capitalists have to be overthrown and then crushed, under the Dictatorship of the Proletariat.

That is *not* how the narrators see this:

"It would completely change how we think about who can become President, the balance of power between the branches of government. It is a reminder that the interpretations of the law, by these nine justices, have real consequences, effecting peoples lives. Highlights the importance of an independent, impartial judicial system".

"We need the courts to be fair, the referees, not players in the game. Who gets to draw the line, what kind of infraction, unintended consequences down the road. Slippery slope, like opening up Pandoras box, living through a defining moment in American history. The choices we make now, both as individuals, and as a country, will have consequences, for generations to come. A time for courage, wisdom, to recommit to the principles that this country was founded upon. Who we are, what we stand for, to fight for, for the soul of this nation".

It is strange that the narrators can accurately point out the current revolutionary situation, yet completely fail to grasp the fact that it is just that! Revolutionary!

They then delve into a little more philosophy:

"Raw emotions of Reddit. Struck a nerve. Moment of truth for America. This clash of ideologies, testing our institutions. The future is what we make it. The choices we make, both individually and as a society. A Constitutional crisis, the last chance to save democracy. Or is it a dangerous attempt to overturn the will of the voters? A sense of urgency, make your voice heard, feeling uncertain, anxious, even hopeless. Uncharted territory. Feeling of impending doom, what ever happens, the consequences will be huge".

It is good to know that people are expressing themselves on Reddit. That is an "American social news aggregation", according to the internet. For that reason, it is best to follow Reddit.

Aside from that, the "Constitutional crisis" to which they refer, is incorrect. Instead, it is a crisis in capitalism. Yet because of their middle class view point, they are not capable of understanding this. Sad!

They then end the video with a combination of philosophy and fatalism. Perhaps it is their idea of being profound:

"No matter what, things are going to change, and not necessarily for the better. We still have a choice, we can sit back and watch, or we can engage, do something, to learn more, to have a conversation, to support the causes that we believe in, to call our Representatives, to join those peaceful protests, to use our voices to demand something better. Think critically with our heads and our hearts, with empathy for all those around us. The future of this country is in the hands of all of us. What will your role be in shaping the future of America"?

Of all the strange statements these middle class people have made, perhaps the strangest is that of having a "conversation". We are clearly on the eve of a Second American Revolution, and they are suggesting that we "talk about it"!

Now is the time for action. Now is the time to demand that the monopoly capitalists abide by their own laws, as stated in the Constitution. They must be held accountable.

Now is the time to *raise the level of awareness* of the common people, the workers and family farmers, to the level of *class conscious people!* That is precisely where the Fourteenth Amendment comes into play! By demanding that the multi billionaires abide by their own laws, the common people will soon learn, from experience, that those same people are in charge, and fully intend to remain in charge!

Without doubt, there is a "time and place" for peaceful protest. Equally without doubt, there is also a time when it is necessary to *abolish* a government, one which does not represent the common people! That happened before, in 1776, and is about to happen again! Americans have done it before, and are about to do it again! As is their right!

Now is the time for true Marxists, Scientific Socialists, Communists, those who call for the Dictatorship of the Proletariat, to become ever more active. As common people are focused on the "Fourteenth", we must use this struggle, of the working people, to raise their level of awareness. Feel free to use the internet, or "social media", assuming that is the correct technical term, to spread the message.

The revolutionary theories of Marx and Lenin must be made available to the working people! That is no where near as difficult as it used to be. Such revolutionary works are readily available, on the internet. As well, most common people are now literate. They must be encouraged to read the Communist Manifesto, by Marx and Engels. Then there are the Essential Works of Lenin, including State and Revolution, Imperialism, the Highest Stage of Capitalism, What Is To Be Done?, and Left Wing Communism, An Infantile Disorder. A proper understanding of those works, will give working people a fine grounding in revolutionary theory.

CHAPTER 4

Fourteenth Amendment Versus the Twelfth Amendment

As stated in my previous article, the Fourteenth Amendment to the Constitution is being used, in an attempt to stop Trump from being sworn in as President, on January 20, of this year. In particular, Section 3 of that Amendment is being cited.

That begs the question: Why is the Twelfth Amendment not being used? In contrast to Section 3 of the "Fourteenth", which is open to interpretation, the "Twelfth" leaves no room for any misunderstanding. I have chosen to copy it here:

"Twelfth Amendment to the Constitution

"The Electors shall meet in their respective states, and vote by ballot for President and Vice-President, one of whom, at least, shall not be an inhabitant of the same state with themselves; they shall name in their ballots the person voted for as President, and in distinct ballots the person voted for as Vice-President, and they shall make distinct lists of all persons voted for as President, and all persons voted for as Vice-President and of the number of votes for each, which lists they shall sign and certify, and transmit sealed to the seat of the government of the United States, directed to the President of the Senate;

"The President of the Senate shall, in the presence of the Senate and House of Representatives, open all the certificates and the votes shall then be counted;

"The person having the greatest number of votes for President, shall be the President, if such number be a majority of the whole number of Electors appointed; and if no person have such majority, then from the persons having the highest numbers not exceeding three on the list of those voted for as President, the House of Representatives shall choose immediately, by ballot, the President. But in choosing the President, the votes shall be taken by states, the representation from each state having one vote; a quorum for this purpose shall consist of a member or members from two-thirds of the states, and a majority of all the states shall be necessary to a choice. *And if the House of Representatives shall not choose a President whenever the right of choice shall devolve upon them, before the fourth day of March next following, then the Vice-President shall act as President, as in the case of the death or other constitutional disability of the President.*

"The person having the greatest number of votes as Vice-President, shall be the Vice-President, if such number be a majority of the whole number of Electors appointed, and if no person have a majority, then from the two highest numbers on the list, the Senate shall choose the Vice-President; a quorum for the purpose shall consist of two-thirds of the whole number of Senators, and a majority of the whole number shall be necessary to a choice. But no person constitutionally ineligible to the office of President shall be eligible to that of Vice-President of the United States."

In a previous article, I have documented the fact that the "Twelfth" lays out the procedure to be followed, in all federal elections. Of course, that procedure is not being followed, which means that those federal elections are fraudulent. Perhaps a brief summary of that article is in order:

There is no "Presidential Election", so that the "November Vote" has no legal standing; American citizens have no voice in the Federal Election; There is no "Running Mate"; There is no "President Elect"; There is no mention of any political party; It is the duty of the Electors vote for the individual of their choice, for both the offices of President and Vice President; These Electors are appointed by the states only; The states have no right to meddle in a Federal Election; All state laws which require an Elector to vote for the candidates of a particular political party, are Unconstitutional.

It may be objected, that this is hardly "democratic". To this, I can only respond that you are mistaken. Contrary to popular belief, democracy is not "majority rule". It is a method of *class rule!* Under the American democratic republic, it is the method by which the ruling class of multi billionaire capitalists, technically referred to as the bourgeoisie, have chosen to conduct their rule.

At least, that *was* their method of class rule! But then, shortly after the Civil War of 1861-1865, they decided to change their method of rule. This involved setting up a "Two Party System", in which the American citizens are allowed to choose between the candidates, of one of those Parties, for federal office. The fact that this violates their own laws, is of absolutely no concern to the capitalists!

Indeed, this "Two Party System" has served them well, for a century and a half. They are loathe to part with it!

This brings us to the current "fly in the ointment", that of "President Elect" Donald Trump. His latest "ravings", has raised concerns, within even the most die hard supporters of the capitalists. While much of his babbling is incoherent -What do windmills have to do with whales?- that which can be comprehended, can best be politely described as insane. These include going to war with the country of Panama, in order to seize control of the Panama Canal; Going to war with Denmark, an American ally, a member of NATO, in order to take control of Greenland; Annexing Canada, as the "Fifty First State", while appointing Prime Minister Trudeau as the "Governor".

In an attempt to stop the "Coronation" of Trump, as President -for life?- many members of the "Opposition", have chosen to pursue the "legal avenue" of Section 3 of the "Fourteenth", which is somewhat ambiguous. As opposed to the "Twelfth", which leaves no room for any misunderstanding!

There is a reason for this. They are trying to "play it safe". They are attempting to stop Trump, while at the same time, trying not to antagonize the ruling class of monopoly capitalists, the multi billionaires. That is the reason they are not using the "Twelfth"!

From their viewpoint, the use of the "Twelfth" is the military equivalent of the "nuclear option"! To be used only as an absolute last resort! Reality check! This is time for the "last resort"! The "nuclear option"!

If the 2024 "Presidential Election" of Trump was to be challenged, on the basis of the "Twelfth", it is very likely that the Supreme Court would be forced to rule that it was indeed fraudulent. They would certainly be hard pressed to "pass the buck", as they did on the challenge based on Section 3 of the "Fourteenth". Then again, it is possible that they would "rise to the occasion", and once again, find some way to weasel out of performing their duty!

But assuming the "worst case scenario"- from the view point of the capitalists!-, and the Supreme Court was to rule that the 2024 "Presidential Election" was indeed *fraudulent,* then it follows that *all Presidential Elections,* since the days of the Civil War, have been *fraudulent!* That is not what the multi billionaires want to hear!

Further assuming that all state laws, which require the Electors to vote for the candidates of one of the two mainstream political parties, were to be struck down as Unconstitutional, which is very likely, then that would mean the end of the "Two Party System". The monopoly capitalists would then be forced to change their method of rule! The last thing they want to do!

As a result of this, the more progressive members of the middle class, are attempting to "walk a fine line". Trying to stop the inauguration of Trump, without antagonizing the multi billionaires. That is the reason they are going with Section 3 of the "Fourteenth", rather than with the "Twelfth"!

This attempt to "play it safe", will very likely come to naught. The Supreme Court has just "passed the buck" to Congress, and those elected officials know how to stall. Besides, the Congress is controlled by the Republicans.

Incidentally as I write this, within the city of Los Angeles, numerous fires are raging, out of control. Absolute infernos. There is little the fire fighters can do. Whole communities are going up in flames.

The response of Donald Trump? He sees this as an "opportunity", a chance to score some political points. He is blaming this on the governor of California!

I mention this in order to drive home the point that Trump is a menace, completely self centred, focused only on himself. Completely indifferent to the suffering of others. He must be stopped.

Now is not the time for diplomacy! "Half measures" get us nowhere! The democratic republic must be defended! Now is the time to hit Trump, and the monopoly capitalists who defend him, with everything in our arsenal! That includes the Twelfth Amendment!

May I suggest, to my progressive middle class comrades, that you unite and challenge the election of Trump, in the courts, on the grounds that it violated the Constitution, for the previously mentioned reasons.

As for those who are reluctant to "take such a plunge", may I suggest that you have nothing to lose. The multi billionaires have already determined to wipe out your class, the middle class, as well as the democratic republic. You have no future under capitalism.

By contrast, you have a bright future under Scientific Socialism. After the revolution, after the existing state apparatus is destroyed, and replaced with a different state apparatus, in the form of the Dictatorship of the Proletariat, your skills will be required. A new society will have to be created, and that calls for highly trained professionals. You will be rewarded accordingly.

Now is not the time to be shy! There is no need to wait for the "axe to fall"! Feel free to "go on the offensive"! Encourage your friends, especially those who are attorneys, experts on Constitutional law, to challenge this election, in a court of law. Join the various organizations, which are fighting for their democratic rights. Become a member of a Council, and train people, in preparation for the approaching Insurrection.

If nothing else, at the time of the Insurrection, you will not be a target of the Revolution. The same cannot be said of those who "straddle the fence", attempting to "remain neutral". As we live in a class society, neutrality is not an option! Either you are with the revolutionary proletariat, or you are with the bourgeoisie! There is no middle ground! Choose wisely!

Time is not on our side. One way or another, with or without Trump as President, the multi billionaires seem determined to force a showdown. This is almost certain to provoke an Insurrection. The success -or failure!- if that Insurrection, depends largely upon the actions we take now. The better prepared we are, the better the chances of success.

A Revolution is similar to a force of nature, a hurricane. It does not wait for people to be prepared. It just happens. The best thing we can do, is prepare.

With that in mind, may I suggest that all of our correspondence contain the following slogans:

Prepare For Insurrection!

Prepare For Scientific Socialism!

Prepare For Dictatorship of the Proletariat!

Prepare for Revolution!

Concerning Biden's "Farewell Address To the Nation"

On January 15, 2025, President Joe Biden gave his "Farewell Address to the Nation". As a great many working people were watching this "Farewell Speech", and were very likely confused, this calls for an explanation.

One of the professional narrators referred to this speech as being very "dark", as it refers to an "Oligarchy taking shape in America". She mentioned that Biden is of the opinion that this Oligarchy, has given rise to a "dangerous concentration of power in the hands of a very few ultra wealthy people".

That is one way of putting it! The lengths some people will go to, in order to avoid any reference to the existence of classes!

True, an American Oligarchy does exist. By definition, this is a "small group of people having control of a country, organization, or institution". This "small group of people", which controls the country of America, are composed of a very few "ultra wealthy people", as President Biden so delicately phrased it. This is to say that those people have wealth in the *tens and hundreds of billions!* Even that is *not enough!* They *want more!* They want to be *trillionaires!*

It should be noted that middle class people are well aware of this, as they are class conscious. It is working class people, proletarians, who are not aware of this, as conditions of life, of the proletariat, do not lead to the awareness of themselves, as a class, with their own class interests.

As that is the case, and as I am mainly concerned with the working class, I should mention that the industrial revolution gave birth to two new classes. At that time, the merchants who lived in town, referred to as "burghers", saw an opportunity to invest their money, and make a great fortune. They succeeded, beyond their wildest dreams!

In the process of investing their money, the name "burgher" became transformed to "bourgeois". At the same time, their money, or wealth in any other form, became known as "capital". For that reason, the bourgeois also became known as "capitalists", a name they generally hate, for some reason. They prefer to refer to themselves as "entrepreneurs".

On the one hand, these freshly minted capitalists invested their money in building factories, mills, mines and such. This is now referred to as the "point of production". They also invested in railroads and shipping lines, or the "means of transportation". And of course, there were the banks, or "financial institutions", possibly the most profitable of all investments.

But then, as no class can live in isolation, a second class of people was created. This class, which has nothing to sell but their labour power, is referred to as the "antipode" to the capitalist class. They are referred to as the working class, or "proletariat". A second revolutionary class! And in fact, the *only* class that is *consistently revolutionary!*

The capitalists who are now referred to as the "ultra rich", or "monopoly capitalists", those with *at least tens of billions,* or even *hundreds of billions,* are now referred to as the "bourgeoisie".

By contrast, those with a paltry few million, or even a "mere" billion or two, are referred to as "middle class" or "petty bourgeois". As the monopolies become ever stronger, ever more complete, the middle class is gradually being wiped out. Those few survivors, of the middle class, are now "living on borrowed time".

There is a reason that I mention this. It is important for the working people to learn certain technical terms. If we are not aware of this, then the capitalists will use our lack of knowledge against us.

It should be noted that the newly created, revolutionary capitalist class, turned into its opposite, completely "reactionary", at the point when capitalism reached the stage of monopoly. This happened at about the beginning of twentieth century. This monopoly capitalism, the "highest stage of capitalism", is technically referred to as "imperialism".

Even the highly respected, self proclaimed "Independent Socialist", Senator Sanders, is now issuing warnings against the "American Oligarchy", rather than against the American bourgeoisie. Yet to refer to them as an "Oligarchy", is an improvement over the term which was common place during the Occupy Movement, of recent memory. At that time, they were referred to as the "one percent". If nothing else, the word "Oligarchy" is a bit more accurate. A step in the right direction!

It is significant that President Biden does not write his own speeches. Instead, he has a professional writer compose his speeches. Biden merely recites those speeches, reading from a tele prompter. As he is very likely suffering from dementia, that is probably the best he can manage.

From the text, it is clear that the "handlers" of Biden are concerned with the fact that the "Oligarchs" are about to seize power. This shows a certain democratic sense, on their part. They are concerned that the American Empire is about to collapse. Their concerns are well grounded!

This fear is quite wide spread, among middle class intellectual narrators. Indeed, some are comparing this to the situation within the Roman Empire, at the time when Rome ceased to be a Republic, and instead, became a Dictatorship. It was the beginning of the end of the Roman Empire.

It is reasonable to expect a certain number of these middle class, somewhat progressive intellectuals, to see the "writing on the wall", and to "jump ship". It is clear that monopoly capitalism has "had its day". There is no point in even attempting to "patch it up", as Biden suggested. It is beyond repair.

In the Communist Manifesto, Marx and Engels foretold this:

"Finally, in times when the class struggle nears the decisive hour, the process of dissolution going on within the ruling class, in fact within the whole range of old society, assumes such a violent, glaring character, that a small section of the ruling class cuts itself adrift, and joins the revolutionary class, the class that holds the future in its hands. Just as, therefore, at an earlier period, a section of the nobility went over to the bourgeoisie, so now a portion of the bourgeoisie goes over to the proletariat, and in particular, a portion of the bourgeois ideologists, who have raised themselves to the level of comprehending theoretically the historical movement as a whole.

"Of all the classes that stand face to face with the bourgeoisie today, the proletariat alone is a really revolutionary class. The other classes decay and finally disappear in the face of modern industry; the proletariat is its special and essential product".

Without doubt, the "class struggle" is now near the "decisive hour". The suffering of the working class is at appalling levels. Countless people are homeless, the more "fortunate" living in cars. Drug overdoses are widespread. Gang violence has led to mass shootings, almost on a daily basis. The police have been reduced to documenting the slaughter. Unemployment is epidemic, as there are simply no jobs. A sense of despair is the rule, not the exception. And the wealth of the multi billionaires, the bourgeoisie, is sky rocketing!

That is the very definition of a revolutionary situation! Now we can expect a "small section of the ruling class to cut itself adrift, and join the revolutionary class, the class that holds the future in its hands".

It is only reasonable to expect that this "small section", will be among the most intelligent of the intellectuals. As the bourgeoisie is determined to wipe out the middle class, they have no future under capitalism. On the other hand, they have a bright future under Scientific Socialism, in the form of the Dictatorship of the Proletariat. Their skills in organization and administration will be in high demand. They will be paid accordingly.

To those middle class, somewhat progressive, more intelligent intellectuals, I have a little word of unsolicited advice. Act now! Do not wait for the "axe to fall"! Trump and his "buddies" -the three richest men in the country!- are determined to "force the issue"! To provoke an uprising! Revolution!

Among other things, they plan to deport *all* illegal immigrants, *along with their children,* including those who were *born in America!* Even though such children are *American citizens by birth,* according to the Constitution, that makes no difference. As far as Trump and his "ultra rich buddies" are concerned, the Constitution is a mere *scrap of paper!*

Further bear in mind that Trump recently told his supporters to vote for him, *one last time!* As soon as he is sworn into office, he fully intends to set himself up as "President For Life"! Dictator!

It has been suggested that Trump was "merely joking". True, the man does have a sense of humour. His idea of being "funny", involves mocking those who are physically or mentally handicapped! Take him at his word! He means what he says!

The collapse of the "American Empire", is the least of your worries! That is a given! Of far more concern, is the attack on the democratic rights of all Americans!

Trump thinks that he can do whatever he wants, and get away with it. After all, he has been doing precisely that, all his life. Thirty four felony convictions, and no penalty! Who can blame him for thinking that way?

Yet Trump is about to receive a "rude awakening"! Americans are prepared to take only so much! They have a proud history of revolution! In fact, their country was founded on revolution! They call it the Revolutionary War! A Second Revolutionary War is about to take place! Donald Trump is about to learn, that which King George learned, many years ago!

At that time, the American Revolutionaries treated the "Loyalists", those who supported King George, to the rather uncivilized practice of "tar and feathers". This public humiliation, of those referred to as "Tories", served to break the power, the "spiritual bonds", of those people. It is entirely possible that such techniques will be used, once again, in the forth coming revolution.

Time is not on our side! Trump and his "ultra rich buddies", seem determined to "force the issue"! So be it! Embrace the revolutionary theories of Marx and Lenin! Bring this awareness to the working class! Take part in Councils! Train, arm and equip the members of those Councils! Be active! Do not wait for the multi billionaires to drive you into bankruptcy, and the ranks of the proletariat!

As well, do not neglect your intellectual friends. Encourage them to also become active. Challenge the 2024 "Presidential Election", on Constitutional grounds. Fight the bourgeoisie on various "fronts". Give them no peace!

Your correspondence should also contain certain expressions, which may become slogans:

Prepare For Insurrection!

Scientific Socialism!

Dictatorship of the Proletariat!

Revolution!

CHAPTER 6

Trump Once Again President

On January 20, 2025, Donald Trump once again took the oath of office, as President, to "preserve, protect and defend the Constitution of the United States". Donald Trump also, once again, immediately broke that oath of office! True to his word, on that same day, he signed various executive orders, including that of mass deportations of "illegal immigrants", including those who are *"American citizens by birth"! In direct violation of the Constitution!*

On the "bright side", so to speak, the opposition to Trump, and his completely reactionary agenda, is spreading, becoming ever stronger. Ever more broad sections of the population are becoming involved. The "Women's Protest March", of 2017, has been replaced by the "People's March", of 2025. Although the number of people taking part in these Marches was less than in 2017, partly as a result of the deep cold, it is now broader and deeper. The mass movement is now no longer gender specific.

The press is reporting that thousands of people, from all across the country, from all ages and backgrounds, came to DC, to protest the inauguration. They are reported to represent over one hundred different "resistance" groups. Clearly, the mass revolutionary movement, the "opposition" has risen, to a whole new level!

This opposition has even extended to the upper stratum of the middle class, the "petty bourgeois". Their concern with the election of Trump, as well as other "recent events", is perhaps best illustrated in a video posted by

Robert Reich, a highly respected economist, author and professor. As it is so instructive, I have chosen to document it here. It provides us with a very clear cut example of the thinking process, including the delusion, of the petty bourgeois.

The fact is that a "small section of the ruling class" is about to "cut itself adrift", and "join the revolutionary class, the class that holds the future in its hands", according to the Communist Manifesto. This "small section" will no doubt include the more intelligent, progressive members of the middle class, those who are destined to join the "revolutionary class", the proletariat, as that is the "class that holds the future in its hands".

The following video exposes the entire range of thinking of the petty bourgeois:

"If you are feeling despair over Trump's Second Regime, I completely understand. Yet I am still hopeful about America. There are ample reasons for despair, but Trump's second term is exposing a reality that has been hidden from most Americans: the raw stinking power of the American Oligarchy, and its use of obscene wealth to gain this power".

As a well educated member of the middle class, the author is supremely well aware of the existence of classes. Yet he chooses to refer to the "upper class", the monopoly capitalists, the multi billionaires, the bourgeoisie, as the "Oligarchy"! As if classes do not exist!

Perhaps this can best be explained by the fact that, as Lenin stated, "the middle class is the most patriotic class". As a patriotic American citizen, the author refuses to face the fact that classes exist, and that there is a war going on between the classes. That war is about to break out into open hostilities!

Now to return to his video:

"My hope is founded on Americans seeing and responding to this reality. Trump is planning another giant tax cut for the wealthy. To pay for it, he is giving two billionaires…the ability to target programs average Americans rely on. He's putting billionaires in charge of key departments. Meanwhile,

CEO's are descending on Mar a Lago, like moths to a flame, in order to curry Trump's favour…"

The author has a fine grasp of the current situation! If anything, he understates it. Perhaps it would be more accurate to state that those are "multi billionaires", worth tens and even hundreds of billions! By comparison, Trump is a pauper! Worth a "mere" few billion! He is a puppet in their hands! They are not going to Mar a Lago to "curry favour"! They are going there to "pull his strings"! Trump in turn is "putting billionaires", these unelected officials, "in charge of key departments"!

Now to proceed:

"The richest person in America, has turned his giant media platform, X, into a cesspool of lies and bigotry, in support of Trump. The second richest person in America, and owner of Amazon, has reportedly agreed to pay $40 million to Melania Trump, for which she's executive producer. Previously, (he) blocked the newspaper he owns, the Washington Post, from endorsing Kamela Harris, in the 2024 election…. The third richest person in America, has chosen to allow lies and bigotry on FaceBook and Instagram, presumably in support of Trump. He says the deciding factor for doing this, was the "cultural tipping point" of Trump's election. And this is just the beginning, of the oligarchic takeover under Trump".

Excellent! The author just exposed a few of the lies and deception, the method of rule, of the ruling class of bourgeoisie! Including out right bribery! Precisely what the working people have to hear! So what does he conclude from this?

"So why am I hopeful? Because Americans do not abide aristocracy. We were founded in revolt, against unaccountable power and wealth. We will not tolerate this blatant takeover".

Once again, most excellent! It is most emphatically true that "Americans do not abide aristocracy"! It is also true that America was "founded in revolt", against the British Empire, in the Revolutionary War of 1776! It happened once before, and it is about to happen once again! A Second Revolutionary War! After all, the American "founding fathers" have thoughtfully given all

Americans the right to "abolish any government", which does not represent them. This right is enshrined in the Declaration of Independence.

Rest assured, the current government is in the hands of the multi billionaires, currently referred to as the "Oligarchy". In fact, they are members of the class of people known as the bourgeoisie. So what is his recommended course of action?

"There will be a backlash, and we will respond, by helping our communities, and protecting the most vulnerable. And we will also respond in the 2026 midterms, and the 2028 presidential elections, by electing true leaders, who care about working people, and the common good. And just as we did at the end of the First Gilded Age, when the oligarchy revealed its hubris and grandiosity, we will demand and get fundamental reforms. Big money out of politics, higher taxes on the wealthy, to pay for what most Americans need. Busting up giant corporations, regulating big finance, holding huge social media platforms, accountable to the public".

Reforms! Fundamental reforms, no less! Could it be that this highly respected writer, this economist, is not aware that we live under a state of monopoly capitalism, technically referred to as imperialism? Is it possible that he is also unaware that "imperialism is reaction, right down the line", according to Lenin? In fact, this is made quite clear in his excellent article, Imperialism, the Highest Stage of Capitalism.

Yet our esteemed author has visions of "busting up giant corporations", presumably as a means of reverting to a state of pre monopoly capitalism. Reality check! That is not about to happen! The monopolies are here, and they are not going away. On the contrary, they are growing, becoming ever bigger, ever more complete, ever stronger. No amount of pious wishes is going to change that!

That being said, it is certainly true that "there will be a backlash". Yet that will involve something more than "helping communities", and the "most vulnerable". Just as in 1776, the working people are about to rise up, to over throw the corrupt government, which does not represent them.

The Second American Revolution will "kick off" with an Insurrection, a popular uprising, just as it did in 1776. At that point, the existing state apparatus, which has been set up by the monopoly capitalists, the bourgeoisie, in order to crush the "lower classes", especially the working class, the proletariat, will be destroyed.

A new state apparatus will then be established, in order to crush the "desperate and determined" resistance of the bourgeoisie, as they make every effort to restore their "paradise lost", as per Lenin. This new state apparatus is referred to as the Dictatorship of the Proletariat, the true form of Scientific Socialism.

The distinguished author then finished his presentation, with that which can only be described as a "flight of fantasy". I have chosen to include it, as an example of how even the best of the bourgeois intellectuals, can fall into errors:

"On the path we were on, the sludge had been thickening, even under Democratic administrations, There were fundamental systemic flaws that remained unaddressed, inequalities have continued to widen, corruption and bribery have worsened. We were on the way to losing our democracy, without even knowing it".

As this distinguished economist refuses to acknowledge the existence of classes, it follows that he also refuses to acknowledge the fact that we live in a class society. Further, the monopoly capitalists have thoughtfully simplified the class struggle. On the one hand, we have the bourgeoisie, and on the other hand, the proletariat. All other classes, such as the family farmers, or peasants, as well as the middle class, the petty bourgeois, have been reduced to the point that they have no great political power, at least here in North America.

As that is the case, the two mainstream political parties, the Republicans and the Democrats, *serve the same class!* They are both *bought and paid for by the bourgeoisie!* To portray the Democratic Party as "progressive", is pure nonsense!

The economist ended his video with an attempt at pacifist philosophy:

"But as a friend put it, authoritarian forces have been building for years, like the pus in an ugly boil. The only way we work up enough outrage to lance it, is for the boil to get so big and ugly that it disgusts all of us. A few years of another Trump regime, even more disgusting than the first, will be hard on many. We cannot gloss over the magnitude of the suffering that will occur. But when the Oligarchy that controls us is exposed for what it is, the nation will see more clearly than ever before, that we have no alternate other than to take back power. Only then can we continue the real work of America: The pursuit of equality and prosperity, for the many, not the few".

This is rather sad. Typical, for the petty bourgeois, but sad. He started the video with a rather accurate description of the current situation, even though devoid of class content. This was followed by documenting a few details of the method of rule, of the bourgeoisie. He even made a reference to the Revolutionary War of 1776, which gave birth to America. Then he suggested a policy of paltry reforms, and concluded with a summary which can best be described as pacifist. Non violent. As he put it, "when the Oligarchy is exposed", then the "nation will see" that it will have to "take back power".

It is a fundamental tenet of Marxism, that the working class is not aware of itself, as a class, with its own class interests. The conditions of life, of the proletariat, do not lead to that awareness. It is up to class conscious members of the middle class, the petty bourgeois, to bring that awareness to the proletariat. That makes so much more sense than enduring "a few years of another Trump regime", in order to "expose the Oligarchy for what it is"!

This video, by one of the finest of the bourgeois intellectuals, is rather typical. We can compare this to a statement, by a dedicated British imperialist, which Lenin quoted in his article, Left Wing Communism, An Infantile Disorder. That statement started by stating the facts accurately, but then fell into fantasy. As Lenin wrote:

"It may be said, in passing, that this argument shows in particular how muddled even the most intelligent members of the bourgeoisie have become, and how they cannot help committing irreparable blunders. That, in fact, is what will bring about the downfall of the bourgeoisie. Our people however, may commit blunders, (provided of course that they are not too serious and are rectified in time) and yet in the long run, will turn out to be the victors".

We can only hope that the progressive, more intelligent members of the middle class, who choose to "cut themselves adrift", and join the revolutionary proletariat, will be able to avoid making those "irreparable blunders". I can only stress the importance of thinking in class terms!

The fact is that the approaching Second American Revolution, will lead to the destruction of the existing state apparatus, and the over throw of the ruling class of bourgeoisie. It will give birth to a system of Scientific Socialism, in the form of the Dictatorship of the Proletariat.

We will know that we are getting our message across, when the Leftist videos, posted on the internet, contain calls for:

Insurrection!

Scientific Socialism!

Dictatorship of the Proletariat!

Revolution!

CHAPTER 7

An Open Letter To Independent Socialists

The American democratic republic is under attack. Now that Donald Trump is once again President, he has wasted no time in implementing his completely reactionary agenda, referred to as Project 2025.

Barely one week into his second term, he has already made several attempts to "terminate the Constitution", with his executive orders. As one Leftist journalist pointed out, "Trump has provided ample ammunition for a third impeachment"! This journalist is referring to the fact that, on "day one" of his administration, he first violated the Fourteenth Amendment, nullifying birth right citizenship, by ordering the deportation of American citizens. Then, he ordered the state of California to amend their election laws. The penalty for not doing so, is to *withhold* federal money, for the severe losses the state suffered, due to the brush fires, within the city of Los Angeles. A clear example of "election tampering"!

It is noteworthy that twenty two states have gone to federal court, in an effort to stop Trump's "birth right citizenship order". A Leftist journalist documented this in a fine article:

"Today, a federal judge, who has been on the bench for forty years, and was appointed by Reagan, just told Trump, and his administration, and his DOJ lawyers, who went into court to argue in favour of that executive order, that it is blatantly Unconstitutional, and issued a temporary restraining order to block it". As the judge stated, "I have been on the bench for four decades. I cannot remember another case where the question presented was as clear".

A second Leftist narrator added that the same Judge "scolded the Justice Department attorney", by stating that "I have difficulty understanding how a member of the Bar can state unequivocally that this is a Constitutional order. It boggles my mind". The narrator then went on to state that he was "Surprised that the judge has not sanctioned lawyers, really out of bounds for lawyers, a shocking thing to come up with".

Those two narrators, whom I just quoted, may object to being referred to as "Leftist". They may prefer such adjectives as "progressive", or perhaps "democratic", in reference to themselves.

Regardless of the manner in which they choose to classify themselves, the fact remains that they have taken a progressive stand, in favour of defence of the American democratic republic. It is significant that they make no claim to being socialist. It is an indication of the breadth and depth of the mass movement, against the completely reactionary agenda of Trump and his handlers, the multi billionaires. It has now extended to the upper stratum of the middle class, the petty bourgeois.

This brings me to the subject of those who consider themselves to be "Independent Socialists", of one shade or another. Such individuals may, or may not, be a member of a particular political party, or of a socialist organization, or both. Yet it is safe to say that all such self described Socialists, are progressive people, at least concerned with people in general, and with the democratic republic, in particular. We can work with such people, as they are honest, people of integrity.

It is reasonable to assume that the vast majority of self described Socialists, are intelligent, well educated members of the middle class, complete with University degrees. As that is the case, they are at least aware of the revolutionary theories of Marx and Lenin, as those theories are taught only in University.

More accurately, the scientific theories of Marx and Lenin are not so much taught, as *distorted* in Universities! As all Universities are "bought and paid for", by the bourgeois, this is perhaps not too surprising.

Yet as those who refer to themselves as "Socialists", are predominantly honest, I am convinced that they are prepared to listen to the "voice of sweet reason". If nothing else, feel free to keep an open mind.

Bear in mind that Marx was, first and foremost, a *Social Scientist*. This is to say that Marx examined society from a *scientific* view point. The fact is that society develops according to certain *laws,* and not according to a haphazard assortment of random thoughts! Regardless of how pleasant those thoughts may be! And rest assured, the thought of socialism is indeed most pleasant!

Having said that, let us examine how Marx phrased it, in 1852:

"And now as to myself, no credit is due to me for discovering the existence of classes in modern society, nor yet the struggle between them. Long before me, bourgeois historians had described the historical development of this class struggle, and bourgeois economists the economic anatomy of the classes. What I did that was new was to prove: 1) that the *existence of classes* is only bound up with *particular historical phases in the development of production;* 2) that the class struggle necessarily leads to the *Dictatorship of the Proletariat;* 3) that this Dictatorship itself only constitutes the transition to the *abolition of all classes and to a classless society."*

It should be stressed, that Marx was concerned with something more than capitalism and socialism. Indeed, the "historical phases in the development of production" led to something more than the "existence of classes". It was only at the point that the "development of production" led to a surplus, so that people were enabled to enslave people, a time referred to as "civilization", that classes first came into existence. Slaves and slave owners.

Yet before civilization, in a time commonly referred to as the "Stone Age", society still existed, albeit devoid of classes. At that time too, society developed, but still according to certain laws, based upon the "development of production".

It was an American anthropologist, Lewis Henry Morgan, who wrote a book in 1877, titled: Ancient Society: Researches In the Lines of Human Progress From Savagery Through Barbarism To Civilization.

Morgan made it abundantly clear, in that book, that society develops "as the product of successive enlargements of the sources of production, which were then reflected in changing family forms".

Marx most emphatically agreed! For that reason, he planned to write an article, based at least in part, on that book. He even wrote notes on that subject.

As Marx stated: "Social relations are closely bound up with productive forces. In acquiring new productive forces, men change their mode of production, and in changing their mode of production, in changing the way of earning their living, they change all their social relations. The hand mill gives you society with the feudal lord; the steam mill society with the industrial capitalist".

Yet before he could complete that work, Marx died, in 1883. So his close friend, Friedrich Engles, carried on the work that Marx was able only to start.

As Engels stated, "Marx had made it one of his future tasks to present the results of Morgan's researches in the light of his own- within certain limits, I may say our- materialistic examination of history, and thus to make clear their full significance. For Morgan, in his own way, had discovered afresh in America, the materialist conception of history, discovered by Marx forty years ago, and in his comparison of barbarism and civilization it had led him, in the main points, to the same conclusions as Marx."

It should be noted that the "gens", to which Engels refers, are commonly referred to as "clans", in North America. Also, the title "American Indians" is no longer politically correct, as they now prefer to be referred to as "First Nations People".

That is somewhat incidental to the point that Engles was trying to make: "According to the gens (clans) of the "American Indians", organized according to mother right, he discovered the primitive form out of which had developed the later gens organized according to father right, the gens as we find it among the ancient civilized peoples. The Greek and Roman gens, the old riddle of all historians, now found its explanation in the Indian gens, and a new foundation was thus laid for the whole of primitive history."

It is significant that Engels referred to this as a "*definitive* book -as definitive as Darwin's was in the case of biology- on the primitive state of society".

This gave birth to the article that was written by Engles, titled, The Origin of the Family, Private Property and the State. An absolute masterpiece, in my opinion. That is also the opinion of numerous scholars. Bear in mind that it is perhaps more accurate to say that it was written by Marx and Engles.

This is my own personal, less than subtle way, of stressing the fact that society develops according to certain laws, and not just under capitalism. As Engels stated, the same "gens", or clan system, which developed in North America, also developed in Europe. The "old riddle of all historians", the "Greek and Roman gens", was explained by Morgan. Society developed, on different continents, according to the same laws.

Those same laws, concerning the development of society, also apply to civilization. The first classes, slaves and slave owners, gradually died out, and gave birth to the feudal system, with their more complicated arrangement of nobility, Kings and Queens, Knights, landlords, tradesmen and serfs. In turn, the industrial revolution gave birth to capitalism, with two new revolutionary classes, the bourgeois, or capitalist, and the proletariat, or working class.

Just as slavery gave way to feudalism, and feudalism gave way to capitalism, so too, capitalism will give way to socialism. It was Marx who proved this, through his thorough, scientific examination of society.

With that in mind, may I suggest that all Independent Socialists read another excellent book by Engels, that of Socialism, Utopian And Scientific. In that work, he draws a clear distinction between the Utopian Socialists, those who think that socialism is merely a good idea, but probably not feasible, and the Scientific Socialists, those who are aware that it follows from capitalism.

As well, I can also suggest the classics, such as The Communist Manifesto, and the Essential Works of Lenin. These include State and Revolution, Imperialism, the Highest Stage of Capitalism, and What Is To Be Done? Also, I highly recommend, Left Wing Communism, An Infantile Disorder.

It is very likely that most, if not all, Independent Socialists are at least familiar with those books. Yet there is a big difference between the bourgeois distortion of the scientific theories of Marx and Lenin, and the theories themselves. Night and day, in fact!

The Democratic Socialists of America, DSA, has an excellent web site, on the internet. I am sure their goals are at least similar to the goals of all self described Independent Socialists, so I have decided to copy part of their web site:

Who we are

The Democratic Socialists of America is the largest socialist organization in the United States, with over 92,000 members and chapters in all 50 states. We believe that working people should run both the economy and society democratically to meet human needs, not to make profits for a few.

What we do

We are a political and activist organization, not a party; through campus and community-based chapters, DSA members use a variety of tactics, from legislative to direct action, to fight for reforms that empower working people.

It is clear that they are a fine, progressive, Leftist organization. It is just as clear that they are completely misguided. The fact of the matter is that we live under a state of monopoly capitalism, referred to as imperialism, and as such, it is the multi billionaires who are in charge. There is no chance that the "working people" can possibly "run the economy and society democratically to meet human needs".

That point is driven home by a separate video, titled "The Oligarchy's Power Is Waking America".

The two narrators are clearly dedicated capitalists, by no means Leftist, but still, concerned citizens, complete with a democratic sense. They are of the opinion that the "billionaires and CEO's are trying to curry favour with Trump".

In this, they are mistaken. In fact, the "billionaires and CEO's" are the puppet masters who are "pulling the strings" of Trump. They are the "handlers", and Trump merely "dances to their tune".

The narrators referred to these multi billionaires as "current robber barons", in this "second gilded age". It is merely a matter of "following the money", to "get to the monopoly", which is "combined with data", so that "American democracy is undermined".

The video is presented in a very convoluted manner, as the narrators are quite confused, but the point is valid.

It is significant that the narrators mentioned the existence of classes. They referred to the "Oligarchy" as being members of a class of people, being "zero point zero one percent of the population". This is to say that a small fraction of the population, one hundredth of one percent, controls more wealth than the "bottom half of the population". The scientific term for this class of people is bourgeoisie, not oligarchy.

They also pointed out that just one of the richest men in America, put a *quarter of a billion dollars* into the election campaign of Trump. They refer to this as "monopoly power wedded with politics". That is one way of putting it!

They then complain that the "three richest men in the country", were "standing in front of all Republicans", the elected leaders of the country! The narrators were of the opinion that those three multi billionaires were "not there for working class Americans". Really? What was your first clue?

Even though this video is presented in a most disjointed manner, by two dedicated capitalists, it is clear that even they are concerned with the power of the monopoly capitalists. They even mentioned the existence of classes.

Conclusion

I consider *all* Independent Socialists to be my Brothers and Sisters, my Friends, my Comrades in Arms. I say this because all are honest, hard working, law abiding citizens, people who care about other people, especially the less fortunate. As do all Scientific Socialists.

For that reason, I have gone to considerable length to document the fact that the capitalists are, first and foremost, liars. All of their text books are filled with distortions, at best, and outright lies, at worst. It is simply not reasonable to expect anything better from them!

Even the best of the upper middle class, intellectual bourgeois scholars, cannot seem to "think straight"! First they state certain facts, then they become confused, and end up in a "muddle", as Lenin phrased it. But then they are not capable of being honest!

By contrast, all Socialists, whether Independent or Scientific, are honest people. It is also safe to say that, all such Socialists have been misled by the capitalists, to one degree or another.

In particular, American bourgeois propaganda is intense! It sets the standard for lies and hypocrisy! Not too surprising, as the monopoly capitalists, the multi billionaires, the bourgeoisie, can afford to hire the finest liars and swindlers!

Do not be fooled! The fact is that monopoly capitalism is *destined* to give birth to Scientific Socialism! In the form of the Dictatorship of the Proletariat! That was *proven* by Karl Marx!

The capitalists are on the offensive! Those with *tens,* and even *hundreds of billions,* are determined to destroy the American democratic republic! They are "wiping their feet" on the Constitution! Defying it at will! At the same time, reducing taxes on the members of their class! Trump is merely their puppet! Their Stooge! He puts Curly Howard to shame!

Now is not the time to "play doormat"! Now is the time to get active. If nothing else, re-read State and Revolution, by Lenin, this time with an open mind. He wrote that in preparation for the Great October Proletarian Socialist Revolution. We can use that to prepare for the approaching American Socialist Revolution.

Now is the time to transform yourself, to take the "quantum leap", to graduate from an Independent Socialist, to a Scientific Socialist.

Time is not on our side. To paraphrase an old proverb, "Time and Revolution wait for no one"! Just as your ancestors did not wait for their Colonial leaders to give the "go ahead", in 1776, so too, the American public of today, is not about to wait. The Second American Revolution could break out, at any time. The monopoly capitalists are about to "force the issue"!

No one knows which particular "spark" will trigger a popular uprising, an Insurrection. We do know that the better prepared we are, the better the chances of success. Heaven help us if we fail!

That is where Scientific Socialists come in. It is up to them, "conscious people", to provide the working people with the proper leadership.

Now the "ball is in your court", so to speak. As you are aware of the revolutionary theories of Marx and Lenin, it is up to you to bring that awareness to the working class, the proletariat. There is no other way!

We will know that we are being successful, when certain slogans become common place:

Prepare For Insurrection!

Dictatorship of the Proletariat!

Scientific Socialism!

Revolution!

CHAPTER 8

Continuous Attacks On American Democratic Republic

It is just over a week into the second term of the Presidency of Donald Trump, and the "Oligarchy" has wasted no time in implementing their completely reactionary agenda, that of Project 2025.

Clearly, the ruling class of multi billionaires, the bourgeoisie, have decided to change their method of rule. No more democratic republic! Americans are about to be relieved of their duty of voting in elections. A few of the wealthiest members of the bourgeoisie, each worth *hundreds of billions,* have come forward to form that which is referred to as an Oligarchy, a small group of people, to run the country.

They have decided to keep Trump as their figure head President, as he is a proper stooge. In fact, he is in the ranks of Curly Howard, perhaps the finest of the Stooges!

The plan is to further impoverish the working class, the proletariat, while further enriching the monopoly capitalist class, the bourgeoisie. At the same time, the middle class, the petty bourgeois, is to be wiped out.

One of the first orders of business, was to "deal with the Illegals". The "gloves came off"! The Immigration and Customs Enforcement agency, ICE, was given "free rein". No restrictions! They are now allowed to conduct raids on schools, churches and other places of worship. If they even *suspect* someone of being an "Illegal", then that individual is arrested, denied any legal representation, and deported. In direct *violation of the Constitution!*

Trump has also announced his intention to open the Guantanamo Bay "Detention Centre", so that he can "detain" up to thirty thousand people, before deporting them.

The mainstream press is also reporting that Trump just fired at least fifteen Inspectors General, in that which they are referring to as the "Friday Midnight Massacre". That same bourgeois press is also reporting that such a firing is *illegal*, as by law, the President is required to give the Congress, thirty days notice. So much for the "rule of law"!

In addition, wide spread "chaos and confusion" was created, immediately after the White House issued a "vague memo", to "temporarily pause all activities related to obligation or disbursement of all federal financial assistance", that could "conflict with President Donald Trump's agenda". Whatever that means!

The effect was to create a "federal funding freeze", on all "federal grants and loans", to "as many as twenty six hundred programs, within the federal government". This includes such programs as providing food for the Seniors, school lunches for children, food banks, food stamps, Medicare and Medicaid. An attack on the poorest, most vulnerable segments of the population! All because such programs could "conflict with President Donald Trump's agenda", according to a Spokesperson for the White House.

She is so right!

The "agenda" of Donald Trump, is to further impoverish the working class, by cutting any and all social programs, while at the same time, further enriching the multi billionaires, the bourgeoisie, with tax cuts.

The Seniors and school children can go hungry! No food stamps for the poor! Let the food banks run dry! No medical services for those who cannot afford it! No shelter for the homeless! Cut expenses! No mercy!

At the same time, the middle class is to be wiped out. All businesses which are Too Small To Succeed- *all but five, including General Motors!-* are about to "go the way of the dodo bird"! Monopoly capitalism! Imperialism at its finest!

In this way, the government will make it possible to reduce taxes on the multi billionaires, the bourgeoisie. Allowing them to become ever more wealthy, ever more powerful! That is the "agenda" of Donald Trump!

This gave rise to a "huge push back", as the mainstream press so ineloquently phrased it. In fact, there was a nation wide uproar, with opposition coming from various segments of the population.

As many as twenty two states immediately challenged this memo, in federal court, and the Judge issued a "temporary stay", at least until February 3.

In response to this, the White House issued a statement which "rescinds the memo ordering the federal funding freeze", although she was careful to add that "this is not a rescindment of the actual federal freeze, just the memo itself". Whatever that means!

Even a leading Senator spoke out against these federal cuts: "Though the Trump administration failed in this tactic, it's no secret that they will try to find another, and when they do, it will again be Senate Democrats there to call it out, fight back, defend American families. The big question is Medicaid. The White House was not clear whether that was part of the freeze, with 72 million people affected. This is the first win for Democrats in the new Trump era, the party of the middle class".

This Senator is correct when he states that, although the Trump administration "failed in this tactic", they will no doubt "try to find another".

Not that this was a "win for Democrats". It was the mass movement, the revolutionary motion, that stopped these cuts. The Senator merely took credit for this. In fact, both mainstream political parties serve the same class of monopoly capitalists, the bourgeoisie.

This was quickly followed by another White House memo, one which "encourages millions of federal workers to resign". Those who choose to "accept the offer", are being promised eight months pay, as a reward. Those who choose not to resign, are being threatened with being fired.

There is only one little hitch. The President has no authority to make such an offer! Those federal workers who resign, can expect to receive nothing! Trump is merely doing that which he does best. Lying!

It is to the credit of the leaders of the Labour Unions involved, that they are letting their members know the truth. Most of these Union members are determined to fight Trump, to fight for their democratic rights. The power of Unions!

The aforementioned is a sampling of the damage that Trump has wrought, within a mere few days of taking office. All branches of the federal government are at a near stand still. The heads of each branch, including the military, seem incapable of making a decision. They are afraid that any decision they do make, will result in their dismissal.

The mass movement against this attack, on the American democratic republic, commonly referred to as the "Opposition to the Oligarchy", is now very broad based. It includes a great many members of the middle class, those who are concerned with defending our democratic rights. Those people are our allies, on this one particular issue.

When I use the word "our", I am referring to all Socialists, whether Independent Socialists or Scientific Socialists.

The strongest supporters of capitalism, as well as of the democratic republic, tend to be middle class intellectuals, as the middle class is the most patriotic class. This places them in the rather strange position of defending the democratic republic, which the bourgeoisie is determined to destroy! While at the same time, defending the bourgeoisie! Duh!

This in no way changes the fact, that these middle class intellectuals are our allies, on this one particular subject. That of defending our democratic republic. Truly, "politics makes for strange bed fellows"!

Yet it is best to not expect too much from such people. As Lenin pointed out, "even the most intelligent members of the bourgeoisie have become muddled, and they cannot help committing irreparable errors. That, in fact, is what will bring about the downfall of the bourgeoisie".

By contrast, the vast majority of Independent Socialists do not defend the bourgeoisie. They tend to be honest, concerned citizens, but labouring under the influence of the bourgeois ideology. For that reason, they tend to think that socialism may be a "good idea", but simply "not about to happen".

This is an example of bourgeois ideology, which Marx refers to as "spiritual power", having an influence over people. This spiritual power is every bit as real, as that referred to as the "physical force elements of repression". The only difference is that the "spiritual power" is invisible, and for that reason, in my opinion, is far more dangerous.

Allow me to stress the fact that all too many middle class, intelligent, intellectual, Independent Socialists, are under the influence of this bourgeois ideology, this "spiritual power". Largely without being aware of this!

To those people, my Comrades In Arms, I can only suggest that you "break the invisible bonds"! Feel free to face the fact that the bourgeois are liars! Further face the fact that both Marx and Lenin were *Scientific Socialists!*

Marx examined society from a *scientific standpoint!* That included, but was not limited to, *capitalism!* Marx then *proved,* that capitalism would give birth to *Socialism!* Marx further proved that, *after* the revolution, *after* the proletariat seizes political power, the completely reactionary class of bourgeoisie, would have to be *crushed, smashed,* under Scientific Socialism, in the form of the *Dictatorship of the Proletariat!*

Just as Marx predicted, early competitive capitalism evolved into monopoly capitalism, at around the beginning of the twentieth century. The capitalists of the time, knew that something had changed. They did not understand these changes, and really did not care. They just knew that their profits had increased dramatically, or as they phrased it, they were "making money hand over fist". This new stage of capitalism, they referred to as "imperialism".

It was Lenin, another *Scientific Socialist,* who "followed in the footsteps" of Marx. He examined capitalism in its "new and latest" stage, that of monopoly, referred to as imperialism. He determined that imperialism is *not* the "latest" stage of capitalism, but the *highest stage of capitalism!* He documented this supremely well in his landmark work, Imperialism, the *Highest* Stage of Capitalism.

Lenin also determined that, while early, competitive capitalism has *certain progressive features,* such is not the case of monopoly capitalism, imperialism. As he phrased it, "Imperialism is *reaction,* right down the line"!

I mention this, for the sake of my Comrades In Arms, those who consider themselves to be Independent Socialists, which is to say, Utopian Socialists. They are people of principle, capable of honesty, unlike the monopoly capitalists. Such people can face the fact that the multi billionaires are making a supreme effort to starve the Seniors, as well as children of poor people, deprive the poor of medical assistance, further impoverish all working people, in order to further enrich their class, the bourgeoisie.

That same class of people, also take great delight in slandering all Scientific Socialists, also known as Marxist Leninists, or Communists. With good reason, I may add! We are their bitterest enemies! Determined to overthrow them, during a revolution, and then crush them, under the Dictatorship of the Proletariat! The worst nightmare of every imperialist!

In particular, American Independent Socialists should be well aware that revolutions happen. After all, it was the "Revolutionary War" which gave rise to the United States! So to say that "nothing good ever came from any revolution", is to *deny the American Revolution!*

Contrary to what the "Oligarchy" would have you believe, a *Second American Revolution* is about to take place.

Just as a "popular uprising" took place in 1776, in opposition to the rule of the British Crown, which did not represent the Colonials, so too, a second uprising is about to take place, in opposition to the bourgeoisie, which also does not represent Americans.

In contrast to the First American Revolution, which was led mainly by the "propertied classes", the Second American Revolution will be led by the working class, the proletariat. For that reason, the outcome will be somewhat different.

As I have pointed out in a previous article, the forthcoming Socialist Revolution will result in the collapse of the American Empire. The continental United States will break up into a number of separate, Independent, Socialist, Council Republics. Three such republics have already taken shape. These include seven states on the east coast, three states on the west coast, and seven states in the midwest, the industrial heartland of the country.

I use the word "Council", which translates to Soviet in Russian, for a reason. In 1917, the Soviets spontaneously appeared in Russia, in time for the Great October Soviet Socialist Revolution.

So too, these Soviets, or Councils, have also spontaneously appeared in America. Just as these Soviets took power in Russia, after the Revolution, so too, the American Councils will also take power, after the forthcoming American Revolution.

If I can be excused for pointing out the obvious, allow me to state that the next American Revolution is about to replace imperialism, monopoly capitalism, with Scientific Socialism!

All Independent Socialists are welcome to take part in this historic event. First, face the fact that you are under the influence of the bourgeois ideology, the spiritual power, of the bourgeoisie. Break those "invisible bonds"! To paraphrase Rosa Luxembourg, "you have nothing to lose but your chains"! Embrace the revolutionary theories of Scientific Socialism! Transform yourself into a Scientific Socialist!

The working class, the proletariat, is not "class conscious", aware of itself as a class. It is certainly not aware of the revolutionary theories of Marx and Lenin. Nor is it aware of the fact that it is destined to over throw the monopoly capitalist class, the bourgeoisie. This awareness has to come from an "outside source". In other words, middle class, intellectual, Scientific Socialists. You are that "outside source"!

Now is not the time to be shy! If nothing else, encourage your middle class attorney friends, especially those who are experts in Constitutional law, to challenge the 2024 "Presidential Election", on the grounds that it was Unconstitutional. In direct violation of the Twelfth Amendment! Trump is a fraudulent President! Vance is a fraudulent Vice President! Act now, before it is too late! Before the democratic republic is completely destroyed!

My Friends, much as I regret putting this burden on your shoulders, I can see no other way of stopping the Oligarchy from seizing power.

The working class is about to rise up, to overthrow the monopoly capitalists, with the Oligarchy at their head, in an Insurrection. Yet without the proper direction, this Insurrection could fail. Working people need leaders! Proper leaders! Leaders who will provide the proper direction! That proper direction lies in smashing the existing state apparatus, and crushing the monopoly capitalists, under a state of Scientific Socialism, in the form of the Dictatorship of the Proletariat.

I just received an email, which I have chosen to use, in order to close this article. It is posted under, We the People, Under Siege:

"So ICE set up a hotline where people can call to report undocumented immigrants. But they had to shut it down yesterday because over 90 percent of the calls were reporting Elon Musk".

May I suggest that the other ten percent were reporting the First Lady! Clearly, their days are numbered!

CHAPTER 9

Trump and Tariffs

It is well kno wn that Donald Trump campaigned for the office of President, on the "platform", or the promise, of "reducing grocery prices", bringing "jobs back into the country", bringing inflation "under control", and in general, "Make America Great Again", or "MAGA".

Just how he planned to achieve these "noble goals", is not so well known. At least, not until now. His plan is simplicity itself. It is simply a matter of imposing tariffs! He could not possibly be more mistaken!

As Trump sees it, in the simplicity of his soul, "The higher the tariff, the more likely it is that a company will come into the US, and build a factory, so that it does not have to pay the tariff".

It should be noted that a tariff is nothing other than a tax, on all imported goods, paid for by the company which buys the products, and then passes that added expense, on to the consumer. Higher prices! Inflation! The very thing that Trump promised to reduce!

With that in mind, Trump announced a twenty five percent tariff on almost all products coming into the US, from Canada and Mexico, and a ten percent tariff on products coming from China, starting on February 4. The three largest trading partners, with the US!

To the surprise of no one, with the possible exception of Donald Trump, those three countries responded with tariffs of their own. Imagine that! A good old fashioned trade war! Not at all what Trump had in mind!

Faced with strong opposition to his hare brained scheme, Trump backed down. He announced a "thirty day pause", on imposing tariffs on Canada and Mexico.

As one mainstream journalist phrased it, "Faced with real world consequences, Trump 'blinked'. Many countries have tried various tariff efforts, for many decades, affecting supply chains, products, grocery prices and shipping. A sudden one way effort, which does not tend to benefit the country that started the trade war".

That same journalist then introduced a "Nobel Prize Winning Economist", an expert on the subject, who quickly agreed with the narrator. He stated that such a tariff "effectively becomes a new tax, increasing inflation".

The conversation which followed was somewhat disjointed, but I have attempted to reproduce the gist of it here, as the economist stated:

"There is no US manufacturing sector. The free trade area has been integrated for over thirty years now. Different pieces of cars are made in all three countries (United States, Canada and Mexico), components may cross the border seven or eight times, so that tariffs merely impose costs on our industry. If Canada and Mexico respond in kind, that will further increase costs, more hurt to the US. The countries are mutually dependent. A tariff is crazy! It is an effective tax on neighbouring countries, will increase inflation, will not lower prices. Even the threat of tariffs will raise costs!" That is the professional opinion of a highly respected, bourgeois economist, one of the finest. In his opinion, Trumps plan to impose tariffs are *"crazy"!* All Americans, including Donald Trump, would be well advised to take note!

Yet the Trump plan, that of introducing tariffs, as a means of raising prices to the point that a "company will come into the US, and build a factory, to that it does not have to pay the tariff", may make sense to a great many working people. The implication is that the factory would merely sell its products, within the US.

In fact, this is characteristic of capitalism, in its early, competitive, pre monopoly stage. Although under competitive capitalism, goods were frequently sold abroad.

There is only one problem with this rosy picture. We already live under monopoly capitalism! Imperialism! The "good old days" of competitive capitalism, are a dim and distant memory!

Monopoly capitalism has characteristics which are quite different from that of competitive capitalism, as Lenin explained so well, in his landmark work, Imperialism, the Highest Stage of Capitalism. As Lenin phrased it: "If it were necessary to give the briefest possible definition of imperialism, we should have to say that imperialism is the monopoly stage of capitalism.….. But very brief definitions, although convenient, for they sum up the main points, are nevertheless inadequate, because very important features of the phenomenon that has to be defined, have to be especially deduced. And so, without forgetting the conditional and relative value of all definitions, which can never include all the concatenations of a phenomenon in its complete development, we must give a definition of imperialism that will embrace the following five essential features:

1) "The concentration of production and capital developed to such an extent that it creates monopolies which play a decisive role in economic life.

2) "The merging of bank capital with industrial capital, and the creation, on the basis of 'finance capital', of a financial oligarchy.

3) "The export of capital, which has become extremely important, as distinguished from the export of commodities.

4) "The formation of international capitalist monopolies, which share the world among themselves.

5) "The territorial division of the whole world among the greatest capitalist powers is completed."

"Imperialism is capitalism in that stage of development in which the domination of monopolies and finance capital has established itself; in which the export of capital has acquired pronounced importance; in which the division of the world among the international trusts has begun; in which the partition of all the territories of the globe among the great capitalist powers has been completed."

Allow me to stress the fact that "monopolies play a *decisive* role in economic life". In fact, it is "finance capital" which gives rise to a *"financial oligarchy"*! In America, this small group of multi billionaires are simply referred to as the "Oligarchy"! They are determined to seize power, to destroy the democratic republic!

As well, under imperialism, it is "capital" which is exported, and not just "commodities", as are exported under competitive capitalism. This capital includes such items as factories!

We now have "*international* capitalist monopolies", so that the multi billionaires who control them, are members of different nationalities. The American multi billionaires have no loyalty to America! Their loyalty lies with the international monopolies! They are not the slightest bit patriotic!

The "whole world" has been divided up! They "share the world among themselves"! There is no competition!

As that is the case, consider the "brain storm" of Trump, to "impose tariffs", as a means of "forcing companies to build factories, so that it does not have to pay the tariffs".

Donald Trump is "living in the past"! He actually thinks that he can "turn back the hands of time"! He plans to set the American economy back *one hundred years!* To the time of competitive capitalism! Which can only lead to monopoly capitalism!

As I was wondering if that man even has a brain in his head, I received an email, on that subject:

"Don't try to explain anything complicated to a man who felt it necessary to explain to the nation and the world that the helicopter or the plane involved in the Washington crash should have moved out of the way."

That answered my question!

Monopoly capitalism is not about to revert to competitive capitalism! The "international capitalist monopolies" are already in existence! As well, the "Financial Oligarchy" is also in existence! They "share the world among themselves"! The American Oligarchy is not about to relinquish their wealth and power! They are not about to allow an independent company to "come into the country and build a factory". This would require the banks to provide the financial backing, which the Oligarchy would never allow.

Placing tariffs on goods coming into the country, would only result in higher prices, within the country. Other countries would in turn retaliate, imposing their own tariffs, giving rise to a trade war.

In conclusion, we can say that capitalism has long since reached its highest stage, that of monopoly, imperialism. There can be no question of reverting to competitive capitalism, or even of "patching up" imperialism. The Financial Oligarchy is focused on enhancing their wealth and power. Nothing else!

The imperialists have to be overthrown, and this can happen only through revolution. The revolutionary movement is growing steadily, and will soon result in an Insurrection. The success of this Insurrection depends largely upon the level of consciousness of the revolutionaries. They have to become class conscious, aware of themselves as a class, with their own class interests, which are diametrically opposed to the interests of the imperialists.

As Lenin made clear, in State and Revolution, the existing state apparatus, which has been set up to crush the "lower classes", must be smashed, and replaced with a different state apparatus, in the form of the Dictatorship of the Proletariat. Scientific Socialism!

As the astute reader may have already guessed, this is my way of giving a broad hint, to middle class intellectuals, who are aware of the revolutionary theories of Marx and Lenin. It is up to such "Conscious People" to bring that awareness to the working class, the proletariat.

For those who are reluctant to "shoulder that burden", may I suggest that you consider the alternative. The Oligarchy has determined to abolish your democratic republic. No more democratic rights! Scrap the Constitution! At the same time, wipe out the middle class. No more small businesses! Only the "Chosen Few", those that are "Too Big To Fail", are to be allowed to survive!

Do not wait for the "axe to fall"! Become politically active!

Take action, before it is too late! Become involved with Councils! Spread the message! Take part in challenging the 2024 Presidential Election, on the grounds that it violated the Twelfth Amendment to the Constitution! Unconstitutional! Trump is a fraudulent president, just as Pence is a fraudulent Vice President. Act now, before it is too late! Before the Supreme Court is abolished! Which is precisely what the Oligarchy has planned!

By contrast, all middle class professionals have a bright future, under Scientific Socialism. We are supremely well aware that it is one thing to run a machine, and something else entirely, to run a business. And under Scientific Socialism, it is necessary to run businesses, not for the purposes of profit, but for that of the common good. That requires the expertise of highly educated, will trained professionals. You will be paid accordingly.

As the working class is quite well cultured now, complete with various digital devices, it is much easier to "spread the word". We have the technology, and would be fools not to use it.

I have long maintained that the best way to educate people, is to entertain them, at the same time. Education through entertainment!

There is no shortage of professional entertainers, in America. May I suggest that such people apply your skills, to the cause of Scientific Socialism. May I also suggest that those same, highly skilled professionals, avoid the use of vulgarity. There is already far too much of that, in the videos on the internet. It is not only disrespectful, but detracts from the message.

I am sure you will do a masterful job. I have complete confidence in you.

Gerald McIsaac

Americans Protesting Against Oligarchy

Barely two weeks into the second presidency of Donald Trump, and the news reports are quite revealing. First he took credit for securing peace in the Middle East, or at least in the Gaza Strip. Now, as a reward for this selfless act, he plans to create a play ground for himself, and the members of his class of multi billionaires, the bourgeoisie. It is simply a matter of "relocating" the two million people who live there, referred to as Palestinians, tearing down the shattered buildings, and "building spectacular developments in Gaza".

Who would have thought that we would ever see the day, that the President of the United States, openly called for *ethnic cleansing? A crime against humanity!*

Yet that is precisely what he is doing! Further, he thinks that he can get away with this. Who can blame him? All his life, he has broken various laws, and not served even one day in jail. This despite *thirty four felony convictions!*

As well, there have been numerous allegations of sexual assaults! Various women can testify to that! These ladies have every reason to feel bitter. They have been denied justice, as the law does not apply to billionaires. Not only that, but they have also been denied financial compensation!

To such unfortunates, I can only respond that nothing can change the terrible trauma that you endured, nor the fact that you have been denied justice. Yet let me add, that now is not the time to "get mad". Now is the time to "get even"! Rest assured, the latter is far more satisfying! It is just a matter of selecting the proper approach.

With that in mind, consider the fact that there are countless videos, on the internet, containing suggestions, concerning the proper course of action. Most of them are of questionable value, at best, but a few of them are rather revealing.

One of the better videos, is titled "President Musk and his assistant Trump have woken a sleeping giant". The narrator, clearly a man with a strong democratic sense, maintains that he "noticed something different over the last couple of weeks…took part in an uprising against Elon Musk's illegal, Unconstitutional power grab, to shutter government agencies, to hijack American data, installing private servers at the Treasury….there is no oversight…He (Musk) has been appointed to a position of great power, that is outside the purview of Congressional oversight, the coequal branch that has a check on the executive branch…..At the Treasury protest, there was a different tone…..shifting…..from general protest to turning on Democrats, demanding Democrats do their job, to be an opposition Party…This is not the moment to find common ground, this is the moment to save the Republic".

This individual is correct, when he states that "something different" has taken place, within the last "couple weeks". That something different is the mass movement, or more accurately, the revolutionary motion, which has increased dramatically. He is also correct when he states that "this is the moment to save the Republic".

Yet his "solution", that of "calling the Capitol Switchboard", in order to express disapproval with the Democratic officials, would have little effect. Those who took part in the Occupy Movement, of several years ago, can testify to the fact that the two mainstream political parties, Democrats and Republicans, serve the same class. That class is the monopoly capitalist class, the multi billionaires, currently referred to as the Oligarchy, technically referred to as the bourgeoisie.

Yet the title of his article, in which he refers to "waking a sleeping giant", exposes an awareness on his part, that the revolutionary motion has now spread to all segments of American society.

A second video is perhaps a bit more pro active. It is titled, "American citizens protest Elon Musk hijacking US Treasury".

The narrator says he took part in a protest, against that which he referred to as "Donald Trump's dangerous agenda, a man who inserted Elon Musk into the actual functioning of the government. They have forced out Treasury officials, overtaken payment systems within the Treasury Department, and in the absence of Congress actually stepping up to do something, citizens are exercising their First Amendment rights, under the Constitution, to redress their government, and express their displeasure and outrage over what is taking place. If you are not able to join in movements like this, in uprisings like this, you find a local group to express your displeasure. It is going to take citizen action, to get anything done, to actually make some change here, so get ready for a fight. People have woken up".

In this, he is correct, when he states that it is going to take "citizen action", in order to "make some change here". He is also correct, when he says that people should join "local groups". These groups are known as Councils, many of which are working "underground", and are preparing working people for the approaching Insurrection.

This was followed by a speech, by a Democratic Senator. He made the appropriate noises, as was expected from a member of the "opposition Party". As it was so completely meaningless, there is no need to repeat it here.

The only surprise was when he stated that "people have woken up", and further, "We have to reach out to everyone in this country, conservatives, liberals, republicans, democrats, and tell them that we have not months, and not weeks, but we have days to stop the destruction of our democracy. In this country, it is the people that rule, not the billionaires, we are taking this country back from Elon Musk."

To think that even a Democratic Senator was forced to admit that "people have woken up"! He also faced the fact that the Financial Oligarchy is determined to destroy the American democratic republic. That is an indication of the strength of the revolutionary movement.

Even the highly respected, self described Independent Socialist, Senator Bernie Sanders, expressed deep concern. He is afraid that the Oligarchy is transforming the American democratic republic into a "Kleptocracy". Yet, in an interview with CNN, he offered no viable method of opposing this trend. Perhaps he has given up?

Incidentally, by definition, a kleptocracy literally means "rule by thieves". It is used to describe governments whose leaders misuse their powers, to steal from their people. It is also referred to as a "thievocracy". An accurate description of events unfolding, within the American democratic republic!

Without doubt, the ruling class of multi billionaires, the bourgeoisie, has decided to *change their method of rule,* from a democratic republic, to a Financial Oligarchy. In the process, they have accelerated the revolutionary motion. The opposition, to this Rule of the Oligarchy, is now broad and deep, extending to almost all classes and segments of society. Even the most dedicated, die hard defenders of capitalism, are expressing their concern. The situation is truly revolutionary!

An Insurrection could break out at any time! The success of that Insurrection depends largely upon the "class consciousness", the level of awareness, of the working class, the proletariat.

Lenin went into this supremely well, in his landmark work, State and Revolution. This was written in preparation for the Great October Soviet Socialist Revolution, of 1917. That revolution was successful, because it followed the advice of Lenin.

In State and Revolution, Lenin stresses the fact that the state apparatus came into existence, with the first appearance of classes. The sole purpose of any state apparatus is to ensure the rule of the class in power, by subjugating the "lower classes". Under monopoly capitalism, it is the ruling class of monopoly capitalists, the bourgeoisie, which subjugates all other classes. To this end, they carefully established a state apparatus, in order to crush the vast majority of working people, especially the proletariat.

At the time of the forth coming American Revolution, we can first expect to see a "popular uprising", technically referred to as an "Insurrection", in which the "common people" rise up and overthrow the ruling class of monopoly capitalists. But then what?

As Lein phrases it, "This course of events compels the revolution *'to concentrate all its forces of destruction'* against the state power, and to regard the problem, not as one of perfecting the state machine, but one of *smashing and destroying it"*. (italics by Lenin)

Lenin clearly stressed the need to *smash* the existing state machine, with good reason. Previous revolutionary experience- the most *bitter* revolutionary experience!- has revealed that if the state apparatus is *not destroyed,* the leaders of the revolution merely take control of that state apparatus, and set themselves up, as the *new rulers!* Out of the frying pan, into the fire!

Yet *after* the revolution, *after* the ruling class of monopoly capitalists are overthrown, *classes will continue to exist!* And rest assured, the former multi billionaires are not about to "resign themselves to their fate". They are not about to embrace a life of "manual labour", as that is merely a "Mexican worker"! On the contrary, they will make every effort to "regain their paradise lost"! They will resort to every lie, deceit, deception, bribery and threat, to return to power! The experience of the *former* Socialist Soviet Union, and *former* Socialist China, leave no room for any doubt!

For that reason, a state apparatus is still required, after the revolution, in order to "crush the desperate and determined resistance" of the monopoly capitalists. But as Lenin phrased it, "It is still necessary to suppress the bourgeoisie and crush its resistance. This was particularly necessary for the (Paris) Commune; and one of the reasons for its defeat was that it did not do so with sufficient determination. But the organ of suppression is now the majority of the population, and not the minority, as was always the case under slavery, serfdom, and wage slavery. And since the majority of the people *itself* suppresses its oppressors, a 'special force' for suppression is *no longer necessary*. In this sense the state *begins to wither away*. Instead of the special institutions of a privileged minority (privileged officialdom, heads of the standing army), the majority itself can directly fulfill all these functions, and the more the functions of state power devolve upon the people generally, the less need is there for the existence of this power. " (italics by Lenin)

Incidentally, this new state apparatus, which exists only under a state of Scientific Socialism, is referred to as the Dictatorship of the Proletariat.

After the successful Insurrection, after the monopoly capitalists are overthrown, after we establish the Dictatorship of the Proletariat, we must avoid the mistakes of previous great revolutionaries, including those of Stalin and Mao. As I have gone into this in previous articles, there is no need to repeat it here.

There is a reason for the sense of urgency, expressed by the bourgeois intellectuals, concerning the attack on the American democratic republic. The fact is that the state of California is now openly calling for separation, from the United States. As well, the state of Texas, the "Lone Star State", may once again form a separate, independent republic, as it once was.

As I have previously documented, the state of California recently formed an alliance with the two other Pacific Coast states, that of Washington and Oregon. It is very likely that those three states will soon separate and form a separate, independent, Socialist Council Republic.

As well, on the east coast, seven state have also formed an alliance. In the midwest, the industrial heartland of the country, yet another seven states have also formed an alliance. Two more Socialist Council Republics, soon to be created!

Truly, the bourgeois scholars have good reason to be concerned! The American Empire is on the verge of collapse! It will soon give birth to several independent, Socialist Council Republics. It is also very likely that those Republics will form a North American Socialist Council Union.

That largely depends upon the American Revolutionary leaders, taking the advice of Lenin. Choose wisely.

Gerald McIsaac

CHAPTER 11

American Republic Close To Collapse

Friday, February 7, 2025. Black Friday! A day which may go down in history, as the beginning of the end of the American democratic republic. The day that American Members of Congress, democratically elected "law makers", were *blocked* from entering several federal agencies. These include USAID, as well as the Departments of the Treasury, Labour and Education. The people conducting the "blockade" were unelected officials, working for DOGE, the Department Of Government Efficiency, led by Elon Musk, appointed by President Trump.

A spokesperson for that group, herself a Member of Congress, warned that "Trump's spending cuts will merely enrich Elon Musk, and harm American families". She gave some excellent advice, that of, "Follow the money. Who they are taking it from, and who they are giving it to. Outrageous. Taking it from our kids, and giving it to billionaires".

Well spoken! In cases of suspected fraud, it is always a good idea to "follow the money". Yet she was careful to avoid any mention of classes. The fact is that the "billionaires", to whom she so delicately referred, are members of a class of people, referred to as the bourgeoisie. They are monopoly capitalists, imperialists, and as such, are completely reactionary.

Particular Members of Congress, those who are members of the Democratic Party, assure us that they are not about to take this, "lying down". Indeed not. After all, it is the Congress that "controls the purse strings". They assure us that the "real fight is still ahead". This is a reference to the March 14 "funding deadline", at which time the federal government will "run out of money", unless the debt limit is increased, once again. Otherwise, the federal government could shut down.

As is well known, the Republican Party has a "razor thin" majority in Congress, with a few of those Members considered to be "mavericks", completely unreliable, if not outright crazy. For that reason, it is thought that the Speaker of the House, Republican Member Johnson, "could be faced with a shutdown, if Democrats withhold their vote".

Consider the fact that the authority of Congress, the legislative branch of government, is being directly *challenged,* by locking the Members of Congress out of key government agencies, and this is the best they can do! Threaten a federal government shutdown, next month, no less! Reality check! Next month may be too late! By that time, Trump may have already seized power, completely! He may just disband Congress, and declare himself to be President For Life! Dictator! As laid out in Project 2025! Wake up!

Now is not the time to sit and wait, to "play it safe". There can be no thought of "straddling the fence". Now is the time to take action, to combine legal with illegal work. We live in a class society, and the class struggle is about to break out, into open class warfare.

Even the most dedicated, middle class intellectuals, although defenders of capitalism, are now deeply concerned with that which they refer to as a "Constitutional crisis". They are convinced that Trump is "wiping his feet on the Constitution", dismantling the democratic republic. And so he is!

On the "legal front", so to speak, may I suggest challenging the 2024 Presidential Election, on the grounds that it violated the Twelfth Amendment to the Constitution. It is the Twelfth that lays out the procedure to be followed, in all *federal elections!* There is no "Presidential Election"! For that reason, Trump is a fraudulent President, and Vance is a fraudulent Vice President. As I have gone into this in detail, in other writings, there is no need to repeat it here.

Allow me to urge all Scientific Socialists, as well as all Independent Socialists, to unite with all those who are determined to defend the democratic republic, no matter how objectionable they may be. Feel free to console yourself with the thought that this alliance is strictly temporary. As well, this individual probably feels the same way about us!

Act now, while we still have a Supreme Court! Tomorrow could be too late!

This brings me to the illegal aspect of revolutionary work, arguably more important. We can learn from previous revolutionary experience, especially from that of the three Russian Revolutions, of the Twentieth Century. That is because the forth coming American Revolution, is almost certain to closely resemble the Great October Soviet Socialist Russian Revolution.

The Russian Revolutionaries of 1917, built upon the experience, of the earlier Russian Revolution of 1905. Even though that Revolution failed, in the sense that the ruling noble family of Romanovs was not toppled, it did succeed in raising the level of awareness of the common people.

At the start of the Revolution of 1905, the common people, workers and family farmers, were mainly honest, hard working, patriotic, tax paying, loyal subjects of His Majesty, Tsar Nicholas. For that reason, when they rose up, in peaceful protest, respectfully asking their beloved Tsar to address their legitimate grievances, they actually expected him to respond accordingly. Instead, he turned the military loose on them. He was not about to allow any discontent!

The 1905 Revolution raged for three years, before dying down, in 1907. Then things quickly "returned to normal", or so it appeared. The nobility, landlords and capitalists, breathed a "sigh of relief". They actually thought, that was the "end of the matter"! It most certainly was not! The "mass movement", the revolutionary motion, had merely died down! Temporarily!

But as Marx pointed out, these revolutionary motions continue to rise up, "ever stronger, ever finer"! And so it was!

Several years later, the revolutionary motion flared up, once again. Yet this time, the common people had no illusions. They knew what to expect. They had been "schooled in the class struggle". They were still patriotic citizens, but not the "loyal and devoted subjects of His Majesty", they once were. Those days were gone! They recognized the Tsar as the butcher that he was.

This, the second Russian Revolution of the Twentieth Century, came to a climax in early 1917. At that time, Lenin was living in exile, in Switzerland, but closely following events in Russia. He wrote five letters, referred to as "Letters From Afar", in late March, concerning those incredible developments. As it is so important, I have chosen to quote it, at length:

"How could such a 'miracle' have happened, that in only eight days…a monarchy collapsed, that had maintained itself for centuries, and that in spite of everything, had managed to maintain itself throughout the three years of the tremendous, nation wide class battles of 1905-07?

"There are no miracles in nature or history, but every abrupt turn in history, and this applies to every revolution, presents such a wealth of content, unfolds such unexpected and specific combinations of forms of struggle and alignment of forces of the contestants, that to the lay mind there is much that must appear miraculous.

"The combination of a number of factors of world historic importance was required for the tsarist monarchy to have collapsed in a few days. We shall mention the chief of them.

"Without the tremendous class battles and the revolutionary energy displayed by the Russian proletariat, during the three years 1905-07, the second revolution could not possibly have been so rapid, in the sense that its *initial stage* was completed in a few days. The first revolution (1905) deeply ploughed the soil, uprooted age old prejudices, awakened millions of workers and tens of millions of peasants to political life and political struggle, and revealed to each other- and to the world- *all* classes (and all the principle parties) of Russian society, in their true character and in the true alignment of their interests, their forces, their modes of action, and their immediate and ultimate aims. This first revolution, and the succeeding period of counter revolution

(1907-14), laid bare the very essence of the tsarist monarchy, brought it to the 'utmost limit', exposed all the rottenness and infamy, the cynicism and corruption of the tsar's clique…those *landlords…who own millions* of dessiatines of land and are prepared to stoop to any brutality, to any crime, to ruin and strangle any number of citizens, in order to preserve the 'sacred right of property', for themselves *and their class.*

"Without the Revolution of 1905-07, and the counter revolution of 1907-14, there could not have been that clear 'self determination' of all classes of the Russian people.…which manifested itself during the eight days of the February -March Revolution of 1917. …

"For the first great Revolution of 1905.… led, after the lapse of twelve years, to the 'brilliant', the 'glorious' Revolution of 1917". (italics by Lenin)

It may be objected that America has not experienced a revolution, such as that of 1905. True! But America has experienced something very similar, which is the Occupy Movement of 2011.

At that time, in America, the common people, the vast majority of whom were honest, hard working, law abiding, tax paying, patriotic citizens, decided to exercise their democratic right to peaceful protest, as is guaranteed in the Constitution. They were merely trying to draw the attention, of their democratically elected leaders, to the glaring inequalities within society. They actually thought that the system was not working properly, but that once this was brought to the attention of the proper authorities, it would be corrected. They could not possibly have been more mistaken!

As is well known, the authorities responded with clubs, tear gas and pepper spray. The tents of the protesters were torn down, with many people thrown in jail. The system was working precisely the way it was supposed to work! In favour of the multi billionaires!

This was a "rude awakening", a "bitter pill to swallow". Just as the common people of Russia had learned, in the previous century, the American protesters learned that they had been lied to, all their lives. It was with the utmost bitterness, that the protesters faced the fact that the ruling class of monopoly capitalists, the multi billionaires, the bourgeoisie, at that time referred to as the "one percent", were in charge, and fully intended to remain in charge!

This revolutionary motion was followed by a time of reaction, as it was in Russia, after the Revolution of 1905.

Now the revolutionary motion has picked up again, but is now "finer and stronger". Those who took part in the Occupy Movement, are now seasoned veterans, tempered in the class struggle. They know what to expect, and are leading this current revolutionary movement.

There are numerous videos, on the internet, produced mainly by bourgeois intellectuals, who recognize the danger, posed by Trump and his Oligarchy. Yet none of them can foresee that the future lies with Councils and Scientific Socialism.

It is significant that, immediately after the Russian Tsar was overthrown, in March of 1917, numerous Soviets, Councils, made their appearance. Up until that time, they had been working "underground", of necessity, as they were illegal. But at the time of the Revolution, they emerged, and were almost as powerful as the Provisional Government!

This is my less than subtle way, of suggesting that Scientific Socialists get involved with Councils. Illegal activity. Train, arm and equip working class people, in preparation for the approaching Insurrection. The future belongs with these Councils.

Gerald McIsaac

Constitutional Crisis

It is to the credit of a considerable number of bourgeois scholars, that they are deeply concerned with the American democratic republic. They are convinced that President Donald Trump and Elon Musk, are determined to overthrow that republic, and establish a dictatorship, possibly even a state of fascism. Which is precisely what they are attempting, as they are following the directions contained in Project 2025. It may help to think of this as the American version of Mien Kampf.

As not all readers are Rhodes Scholars, for the benefit of those who may not be aware, I should mention that there are three branches of the American government. These consist of the legislative, judicial and executive, as per the Constitution. The intent, of the Founding Fathers, was to ensure that no individual or group will have too much power.

Each branch has the authority to respond to the actions of the other two. This is referred to as the "system of checks and balances".

The legislative branch is essentially made up of Congress, which is the Senate and House of Representatives. They make the laws, can confirm or reject presidential nominations for federal agencies, federal judges and the Supreme Court. As well, only the Senate has the authority to declare war, while the House of Representatives controls the money.

For example, the president, as head of the executive branch, can veto legislation created by Congress, although the Congress can also override that veto. Congress can also confirm or reject the nominees of the president. That same Congress can also remove a president from office, although this has never happened. At least, not yet!

The judicial branch is mainly composed of courts, headed by the Supreme Court. The justices of that Supreme Court, nominated by the president and confirmed by the Senate, have the authority to strike down any laws which they consider to be Unconstitutional.

Since the creation of the country, this system has worked reasonably well. Not any more! The multi billionaires, monopoly capitalists, imperialists, the class of people technically referred to as the bourgeoisie, currently referred to as the "Oligarchy", can no longer rule in the "old way". They have decided to *change their method of rule!* That is where Donald Trump and Elon Musk come into play. And make no mistake, they must be stopped!

There are a number of videos available on the internet, concerning that subject. In my opinion, one of the finest is titled, "Judge slaps Trump with brutal criminal warning".

In this video, the narrator does a fine job of documenting the fact that "the whole point of signing a whole mountain of ridiculous, disruptive and illegal executive orders, on day one, was not only to create chaos, but (also) a confrontation with the judiciary".

Remarkably enough, this is very likely the case! Bear in mind that only a madman would deliberately challenge the judiciary! A judge, especially a federal judge, has tremendous power! That power has been given to them, by the Founding Fathers, in the Constitution. To challenge a federal judge, is to challenge the Constitution! Trump is placing himself above the Constitution! The law does not apply to him! He thinks that he can do anything he wants!

According to a legal expert, this challenge, to the judicial system, is "maybe the most critical of our lifetime...our democracy depends upon the courts being able to enforce and interpret the law...Vice President Vance says that 'judicial orders need not be followed'…there is no more control or restraint around the executive…no guard rails…three branches of government turned into one"

The narrator refers to this as "full blown fascism", and "must be taken seriously".

Yet it is also a fact that the courts are taking action. In fact, a separate legal expert is of the opinion that the federal court will "move to criminal contempt…they are going to rule against the administration in that case, and the Supreme Court is going to back them up". We can only hope that is true!

The narrator went on to state that a federal judge, in the state of Rhode Island, has ruled that the Trump administration has defied his ruling, and his order.

Apparently, this has attracted the attention of one of the most highly respected news papers in the country, the New York Times. According to the narrator, he quotes the NYT as saying, " (Judge) McConnell said the White House has defied his order to release billions of dollars in federal grants, marking the first time a judge has expressly declared that the Trump White House was disobeying a judicial mandate. …The ruling by Judge John J. McConnell Jr in Rhode Island federal court ordered Trump administration officials to comply with what he called the 'plain text' of an edict he issued on January 29".

The narrator considers this to be the "initial step to define contempt". This was followed by a further statement, by the judge: "Persons who make private determinations of the law and refuse to obey an order generally risk criminal contempt, even if the order is ultimately ruled incorrect".

This brings us to the "interesting" question, posed by the narrator, as to whether "the US Marshalls will follow through on a court order? This is where the real test of our democracy will come to a head. Our courts lack the legal means of enforcement. They rely on the US Marshalls service, to carry out the will of the court. And guess which branch the US Marshalls service is in? Yes, the executive. That would be the very branch that Trump is purging and replacing with loyalists. Democracy will hang in the balance of that decision".

The narrator could have added that, in order to make the transition, from a democracy to a dictatorship, all officials must first take a different oath, from that of perhaps "preserving, protecting and defending the Constitution", to that of loyalty to an individual, perhaps Donald Trump.

As that is the case, we certainly have cause for concern, especially as he has been busy purging various government agencies, including the Marshalls service. Dedicated, patriotic, hard working Americans are being replaced, with those who are completely MAGA, loyal to Trump, above all else. Or so the Project 2025 people believe!

In my opinion, Trump and Musk have "bitten off more than they can chew"! I personally know a great many Americans, and rest assured, have deep differences with most of them. Not too surprising. Yet I would never accuse any of them of being traitors, people who would betray their country, break their oath of allegiance. I suspect that is true of the most die hard fans of Trump.

I am sure that, if a member of the Marshalls service was ordered, by the courts, to arrest a member of the Trump administration, even Donald Trump himself, then that arrest would take place.

No doubt, a great many readers may wonder why a Scientific Socialist, a Communist, would be so concerned with a democratic republic. Because, according to Lenin, "The democratic republic is the best form of the state, under capitalism. But we have no right to forget that wage slavery is the lot of the people, even in the most democratic bourgeois republic".

As that is the case, it is up to all Scientific Socialists, as well as all Independent Socialists, to unite with all those who are determined to preserve the democratic republic. That includes those who are the most avid supporters of capitalism.

As the federal courts are already taking an interest, preparing to charge members of the Trump administration- perhaps even Trump himself!- with "criminal contempt", then may I suggest that we "add to his burden". More charges! It is the least we can do!

Of course, I am referring to the Twelfth Amendment to the Constitution. That outlines the procedure to be followed in all *federal elections!* As that procedure was not followed, in the "2024 presidential election", then it follows that Trump is a fraudulent President, and Vance is a fraudulent Vice President.

I am sure that all bourgeois intellectuals, with a democratic sense, can agree to work with us, on this one particular goal. That is so much better than fascism.

CHAPTER 13

Council Power

Russia, 1905. The time of the first Russian Revolution, of the Twentieth Century. Also the first time that Councils made their appearance.

In the Russian language, these Councils are referred to as Soviets. For the purposes of this article, as I am writing with Americans in mind, I have chosen to refer to them as Councils.

Contrary to popular belief, these Councils, or Soviets, were not a creation of the Marxists. They were created spontaneously, by the common people, by whom I mean the workers and family farmers, those who are referred to as peasants. As the "mass movement", the revolutionary motion, of the common people gained strength, that same movement gave birth to the Councils.

The Marxists of that time, referred to as Bolsheviks, later referred to as Communists, could not possibly have been involved in the creation of those Councils. The reason for this is quite simple. All such Marxists had been previously arrested, sent to prison, and were either executed, died or had been exiled. Lenin was no exception. He was first sent to Siberia, and only later, allowed to leave the country. Exiled.

In 1905, the Russian Empire was huge, one of the largest, most powerful Empires in the world. For three centuries, it had been ruled by the Romanov family. The Emperor, or Tsar, at that time, was Nicholas the Second, commonly referred to as "Nicholas the Bloody". He believed in "running a tight ship"! He was not one to tolerate any discontent! As he was "appointed by God", he had a rather high opinion of himself. Further, it was his belief that his "subjects" needed a "firm hand". Nicholas was just the man to apply that "firm hand"!

Yet in that same year, the common people rose up, in that which has gone down in history as the "Russian Revolution of 1905". For three years the Revolution raged, and the Romanov monarchy was deeply shaken, but not toppled. At the end of the Revolution, Tsar Nicholas remained in power.

The Revolution of 1905-07, was followed by a time of reaction. All dissent was crushed, with the utmost brutality. The Councils were forced "underground", all but wiped out.

Several years later, around 1910, the mass movement picked up, once again. At first, it was weak, but gradually gained strength. As the revolutionary motion gained strength, so too, the Councils also gained strength.

The Second Russian Revolution, of the Twentieth Century, broke out into open rebellion, in February of 1917, partly as a result of the First World War. As Lenin pointed out, this War served to "accelerate the course of world history".

It is no exaggeration to say that, in February of 1917, the whole world was shocked. Tsar Nicholas was forced to "abdicate the throne". For three centuries, the Romanovs had ruled one of the biggest, most powerful Empires in the world. Now the Tsar was forced to "step down", by the "common people", no less! The power of revolution!

As if that was not "bad enough", it soon became apparent that the Councils, which had been working underground, illegally, gaining strength, were now a force with which to be reckoned! In fact, they were strong enough to challenge the authority of the Provisional Government, of the Kerensky Regime! Almost evenly matched!

This is to stress the fact that Councils do not just "magically appear", at the time of a Revolution, as if a "fairy godmother waved her magic wand". Indeed not. They come into existence as the revolutionary motion gains strength, underground, illegally, before the beginning of open hostilities.

Nor do they always appear, in every Revolution. Yet they are certainly "alive and well" in North America. The experience of the city of Seattle, in which a segment of that city declared itself to be autonomous, the "Capital Hill Autonomous Zone", is proof of that. The Zone was led by a Council.

Of course, that Zone was crushed, with considerable brutality. After all, it was a challenge to the state power, of the monopoly capitalists. By declaring the Zone to be "Autonomous", the revolutionary members of that Zone, were challenging the authority of the ruling class of monopoly capitalists, the multi billionaires, the bourgeoisie. Not to be tolerated!

Bear in mind that, as Lenin said, writing in July of 1917, "Let us not forget that the issue of power is the fundamental issue of every revolution". This is to say, "Which class holds state power"?

On that subject, it is significant that, at the time of the February Russian Revolution of 1917, Lenin was still in exile, living in Switzerland. He was able to return to Russia, in April of that year. To this day, bourgeois scholars cannot understand the reason that the Provisional Government of Kerensky, did not arrest him, as soon as he stepped off the train, in Saint Petersburg.

Because they did not dare! The Councils were that powerful! Immediately after the February Revolution, which overthrew Tsar Nicholas, the Provisional Government was forced to *share power with the Councils!*

Of course, this "sharing" of state power could not last, and did not last. After all, the state apparatus is merely set up by one class, the ruling class, in order to crush any and all subordinate classes. One class must rule! The other class must submit!

In the case of Russia, in early 1917, the situation was further complicated, due to the existence of various classes. These included the nobility, with the Romanovs at the head. Closely allied with the nobility, was the class of landlords, those who took great delight in exploiting the family farmers, the peasants, a different class. Then there was the class of monopoly capitalists, the multi millionaires, the bourgeoisie, as well as the small time capitalists, the middle class, the petty bourgeois. And lest we forget, the one and only consistently revolutionary class, the working class, the proletariat.

As can be expected, these different classes were represented by different political parties, who fought for their best interests. These included the Constitutional Democrats, or "Cadets", considered to be very "Right Wing", as they were deeply concerned with the nobility and landlords. The Socialist Revolutionaries, SR's, were considered to be more "moderate", and represented a great many family farmers. They in turn were divided into "Left" and "Right", with the Left Socialist Revolutionaries closer to the Bolsheviks. Then there were the Mensheviks, those who claimed to be Marxists, but were revisionists.

All of these Parties had a voice in the Russian government, whether in the Provisional Assembly, or in the Councils. If I am not mistaken, they even shared the same building, within the capitol of Saint Petersburg. This is to say that Lenin certainly has his hand full!

There is a reason I have gone into the political situation, in Russia, in the middle of 1917, in detail. Because it bears a striking resemblance to our current situation. Our forthcoming American Revolution will closely resemble the Great October Russian Proletarian Revolution.

That Revolution is referred to as a "Proletarian Revolution", even though the Russian proletariat was in a minority. That is because it was the proletariat that led the Revolution!

By contrast, in North America, the proletariat is in the vast majority. The monopoly capitalists have done -and are continuing to do!- a most impressive job, of wiping out all other classes. It is safe to say that only the remnants of other classes, are still in existence. These include the family farmers, and the small business owners.

The class struggle is now sharp and clear. The multi billionaires, the bourgeoisie, against the working class, the proletariat.

It is my most fervent hope, that those who consider themselves to be Independent Socialists, will take these facts into account. It was Lenin, a true Marxist, a Scientific Socialist, who led the Russian October Revolution to victory, against all the odds. But only because he followed the scientific theories of Marx!

Feel free to take note, Independent Socialists, my Brothers and Sisters, my Comrades in Arms. The only true socialism is Scientific Socialism, as outlined by Marx, as applied to monopoly capitalism by Lenin, and carried through to success in October of 1917, in Russia.

At the same time, face the most unpleasant fact that you have been lied to, deceived, misled, by professional liars. The Universities are filled with such individuals! The best of them are quite charming! Smooth! Sophisticated! Persuasive! With years of experience! Experts at faking sincerity!

There is no need to be too hard on yourselves. Over a period of many years, these bourgeois frauds have mastered the fine art of deception. As they are so highly respected, they are able to exert a certain influence over honest people. The spiritual power of the bourgeois intellectuals! Professor Power!

Now is the time to cast off that spiritual power! Break those invisible chains! Face the fact that Marx and Lenin were correct all along! That the only true socialism is Scientific Socialism!

Now is also the time to stop the Oligarchy, before the democratic republic is completely destroyed. To combine legal with illegal work. To legally challenge the imperialists, in a court of law. To get involved with Councils. To arm, train and equip working people, in preparation for the approaching Insurrection. Illegal work!

Time is not on our side. Project 2025 is currently being put into place. We are very close to a fascist dictatorship. The Oligarchy is wasting no time.

Bear in mind that you have no future, under monopoly capitalism. The imperialists will see to that! By contrast, you have a bright future under Scientific Socialism. Your organizational skills, as well as your training and experience in running a business, will be in demand. As a highly skilled professional, you will be appreciated and rewarded, most handsomely. Any past service to the monopoly capitalists, will not be held against you. Those of us who are Scientific Socialists, Communists, will make sure of that.

That is certainly preferable to a fascist dictatorship.

Gerald McIsaac

CHAPTER 14

Separate American Independent Socialist Council Republics

As stated in my previous article, the next American Revolution will closely resemble the Russian Great October Soviet Socialist Revolution, of 1917. This is because Russia, at that time, was a rather highly industrialized capitalist country, one which had also embraced imperialism. Russia had also subjugated numerous other nations, as has America. The similarities are striking.

After that Revolution, the nations which had been subjugated, by the Russian Empire, achieved independence. Most of those newly independent republics, but by no means all, were able to establish Independent, Soviet, Socialist Republics, in that the word Soviet means Council. These Republics, in turn, came together to form the Union of Soviet Socialist Republics, the USSR.

This is to stress the fact that all of the countries which had been crushed by the Russian Empire, under the rule of the Romanovs, were able to achieve independence, after the Revolution. Yet not all of them were able to establish a state of socialism. Countries such as Poland and Finland became independent, but not socialist. They remained capitalist.

This has certain implications for America.

First let me state that the citizens of the United States, refer to themselves as Americans. Even though the title is not completely accurate, I have chosen to use that nomenclature, out of respect for those people. And rest assured, I have the utmost respect for Americans! They are a fine people, with a history of revolution, of which they can be most proud. Very soon, they are about to build upon that tradition of revolution!

The United States is composed of fifty states, forty eight of which are located on one land mass, referred to as the "Continental United States". The other two "states" are those of Hawaii and Alaska, which are really nothing more than colonies, separate republics, crushed under the American Empire.

Yet there are other republics, which are also crushed by the American Empire. Some of these, such as Puerto Rico, are referred to as "Districts", while others are classified as "Protectorates". At the time of the American Revolution, we can expect all of them to win their independence, just as happened at the time of the Russian Revolution.

This brings us to the subject of the break up of the "Continental States". As I have documented in a previous article, three separate republics have already taken shape. These are composed of seven states on the East Coast, three states on the West Coast, and seven states in the Midwest, the industrial heartland of the country. Yet other separate, independent republics are also taking shape.

Naturally, the mainstream press is doing their best to keep this "under wraps". Yet the "Leftist press", or "underground press", is covering this, as best they are able, posting videos on the internet. This is to say that the journalists are doing a fine job of documenting that which is happening, while at the same time, being completely unable to understand the implications. These bourgeois intellectuals either will not, or cannot, imagine anything beyond a capitalist society. As they are under the influence of the bourgeois ideology, this ideology prevents them from examining the development, from a scientific standpoint. These "blinders" restrict them to the narrow framework of capitalism.

Perhaps one of the finest, most clear cut examples of this, is contained in a video, titled: "California's bold move for independence, could Calexit change the US forever?"

In this video, the narrator documents the fact that California is an "economic power house". He also documents the "quiet but determined wave of discontent", one which "started as a whisper", but has now evolved into a "political movement", which is determined that "California should secede from the United States".

This is very true, as far as it goes. But it does not go very far. It neglects to mention the fact that California has recently formed an alliance with the two other West Coast states of Oregon and Washington. Almost certainly, at the same time that California secedes from the United States, Oregon and Washington will join them, and form a separate republic.

As the narrator sees it, this secession could happen only after overcoming various "legal and Constitutional hurdles", which would involve "protracted legal battles". He was even bold enough to mention the possibility of "federal intervention", a most delicate reference to an invasion by American troops. Another Civil War!

The idea that California could secede from the Union, as a result of a revolution, clearly never occurred to this bourgeois scholar!

Strangely enough, this is not too surprising. Despite the experience of previous revolutions, including the American Revolutionary War, which gave birth to the United States of America, all bourgeois scholars refuse to recognize the fact that revolutions take place! Their capacity for self delusion is most impressive!

Lenin pointed out the fact that, even the best of the bourgeois scholars, manage to work themselves into a "muddle". And this is what will "bring about the downfall of the bourgeoisie"!

This same bourgeois scholar also neglected to mention the creation of Councils, or Soviets, which is taking place throughout the country. Just as happened in Russia, before the Revolution, these Councils are underground, illegal, growing, becoming ever stronger. Also, just as happened in Russia, at the time of the Revolution, these American Councils will emerge, "come to the surface", a militant proletarian organization, a power with which to be reckoned!

The narrator is to be given credit for the fact that he mentioned the state of Texas, which may also soon secede. The "Lone Star State", as it refers to itself, was once a separate republic, and may soon be a republic, once again. A fourth separate independent republic, carved from the Continental United States!

No doubt, these independent republics will come into existence, at the time of the American Revolution. The only question is, will they embrace Scientific Socialism, with Council Power, in the form of the Dictatorship of the Proletariat, or will they remain capitalist?

That largely depends upon the efforts of Scientific Socialists. It is up to such people to raise the level of awareness of the working class. The members of that class, proletarians, must be made aware of themselves, as a class, with their own class interests. Those interests are diametrically opposed to the interests of the monopoly capitalist class, the multi billionaires, the bourgeoisie, currently referred to as the Oligarchy.

This is to say that the working class, the proletariat, must be made aware of the revolutionary theories of Marx and Lenin. As the proletariat is in the vast majority, and well cultured, with access to various digital devices, this is not the "tall order" that it once was.

Allow me to once again, urge all Independent Socialists to face the fact that Marx and Lenin were correct. The "way forward" is through Scientific Socialism, Councils and the Dictatorship of the Proletariat.

The alternative is a continuation of monopoly capitalism, under separate, independent republics. Not a vast improvement.

Gerald McIsaac

CHAPTER 15

Growing Opposition to Trump and Musk

On January 20, 2025, at the inauguration of President Donald Trump, Elon Musk gave the straight arm Nazi salute. It is entirely possible that it was merely a display of exuberance, and not meant to embrace fascism. Yet the actions of Elon Musk suggest that he is a great fan of fascism.

There are numerous videos on the internet, which express deep concern that the American democratic republic is under attack. With good reason, I might add! Because it is under attack! There is even a strong possibility of a fascist dictatorship. That requires an equally strong response, from all of those who are determined to defend democracy, regardless of their political convictions. This includes those who are considered to be very "conservative", or "Far Right", as well as those who are considered to be very "progressive", or "liberal", or "Far Left", or even "Independent Socialists". This is referred to as an "anti fascist, popular alliance", in defence of the democratic republic.

In a time of crisis, those who do not normally associate with each other, tend to come together, against a common enemy. They put aside their differences, even their mutual animosity, at least temporarily, in pursuit of a common goal. This is a time of crisis.

Perhaps an example will be helpful.

Immediately after the Great Russian Proletarian October Revolution of 1917, the country was still at war with Germany and the Central Powers. The Russian army was also collapsing, literally falling apart, as countless soldiers deserted.

As a result of this, the German troops were able to advance, practically unopposed. In this time of crisis, as "desperate times call for desperate measures", Lenin "rose to the occasion", and did that which was normally unthinkable. He requested assistance from the French.

As the French were also at war with Germany, they responded by sending some demolition experts, led by a French officer, a monarchist, a rabid anti Bolshevik. He met with Lenin, and they were civil with each other, even though there was mutual hatred. After all, they had a common enemy.

I can only suggest that all of those who are defenders of democracy, come together, put aside your differences, at least temporarily, and unite against the trend towards a dictatorship, if not outright fascism.

That being said, it is best not to expect too much from these "democratic allies". They are completely restricted by their bourgeois ideology, simply unable to think in revolutionary terms, that of combining legal and illegal activity. Perhaps the finest example of this, is the video titled: "Trump's Sparks Dictatorship Fears With Chilling Declaration".

The narrator thoughtfully presents the story, "from two very different angles". One "angle" is represented by a journalist from CNN, a mainstream news outlet that is considered to be quite "moderate", and the "second angle" from a news outlet that is considered to be quite "Right Wing", Fox News.

The narrator first states that the "breaking news" is that of "Trump signalling his plans to take his authoritarian ambitions to a new and dangerous level".

The journalist from CNN decries the fact that the "mugshot" of Trump, taken at the time he was arrested and charged, "for his efforts to overturn the election", is now proudly displayed, in the Oval Office, of the White House. She clearly thinks this is terrible!

By contrast, the journalist from Fox News considers this to be a "great message"! A "badass mug shot"! (Trump) "channelled the anger of the American people, that the government was weaponized in this way, against a political candidate. We have never seen anything like this, in the United States…something that was supposed to humiliate him, he turned into a triumph". This was followed by a comparison to Christianity! As if Trump is a living, breathing, walking, talking, martyr! The Messiah! Sent to rule America!

This is confirmed by a post, allegedly made by Trump, in which he states that "He who saves his country does not violate any laws". This is similar to the statement, by Richard Nixon, to the effect that, "When the President of the United States breaks the law, it is not a crime".

The narrator then points out that "this is a line straight out of the dictator playbook", a "Napoleonic level delusion". It means that "laws do not apply to him if he decides he is 'saving' America. That's how authoritarians justify everything".

This is followed by a lovely young lady, a "career public defender for fifteen years in Manhattan", who expressed her deep concern, over this "terrifying" post by Trump. She considers this to be truly "dangerous", a true "Constitutional crisis in the making…This is how authoritarian regimes operate….In a democracy, it is supposed to be that no one is above the law…and if someone gets to decide that their actions …are justified, no matter what, then there are no laws, there is no Constitution…no democracy…." She is so right!

The narrator referred to this statement, by Trump, as a "glimpse into the mindset of a madman…the question is who can stand up to stop him…"

In this video, the facts were presently, quite accurately. The more "moderate", progressive individuals, are deeply concerned with preserving the democratic republic. The more "conservative", reactionary, "Right Wing" people, are clearly in favour of a dictatorship, by the Oligarchy, led by Trump and Musk.

The proper question was even asked, that of how to stop Trump and Musk, from establishing a dictatorship. So far, so good. Their answer? To call your Member of Congress!

There is certainly no harm in this, and it is completely legal. At the same time, I cannot help but wonder why they are not also calling for a challenge to the 2024 "Presidential Election", on the grounds that it was Unconstitutional. It clearly violated the Twelfth Amendment, which lays out the procedure to be followed, in all federal elections. A Supreme Court decision, on this matter, in our favour, would serve to clear out the whole "pigsty", currently referred to as the White House.

It is also a fact that the proper Marxist approach, is to combine legal with illegal activity. One such illegal activity, is to get involved with Councils, as happened in Russia, before the Revolution. Working people must be trained, armed and equipped, in preparation for the approaching Insurrection.

There is a second Video, which serves to drive home the urgency of this preparation. That video is titled: "George Conway on defiance of court orders: We are basically a criminal regime".

As the title suggests, George Conway made a few fine points. In his words, he alleges that "Donald Trump is a criminal sociopath…they do not want to obey laws, they don't want to obey rules, they do not think they apply to them,…. Donald Trump has no moral conscience, no empathy, he cares only about Donald Trump… (he maintains) that 'Article two allows me to do whatever I want'. …now we are at stage three, where we are ignoring laws…refusing to spend money appropriated by Congress, which is against the law,….Musk has not been appointed lawfully under the Constitution …now at stage four, where democracy can die…the rule of law can die and Constitutionalism can die…. charges would have to be brought by Trump's DOJ …the legal mechanism… everyone friendly with Trump gets a pass….the Justice Department is the only way the courts can enforce the orders…the marshals service is part of the Justice Department….which reports to Trump,…a lawless criminal…a criminal regime…we will soon be in open defiance".

Considering the fact that these accusations, even though disjointed, barely coherent, were being made by George Conway, is a very serious matter. This is to say that Conway has never been referred to as a "Leftist" person, and would probably be insulted by the suggestion. Yet he is concerned by the attack, on the democratic republic, by Trump and Musk.

He also pointed out the fact that the courts rely on the Marshals service, to carry out their rulings. The fact is that the Marshals service is under the Department of Justice, which answers to President Donald Trump. No wonder Trump is "purging" the Justice Department! Replacing officials who are determined to uphold the Constitution, with those who are loyal only to Trump!

Yet opposition is growing. This is pointed out quite clearly, in another video, titled: "A six resignation kind of day at DOJ, following Trump's sketchy deal with NYC mayor Eric Adams".

In this video, it is reported that, according to the New York Times, the headlines read, "Order to Drop Adams Case Prompts Resignations in New York and Washington". It goes on to state, "Manhattan's US attorney on Thursday resigned, rather than obey an order from a top Justice Department official to drop the corruption case, against New York City's mayor, Eric Adams.

"Then, when Justice Department officials transferred the case to the Public Integrity section in Washington, which oversees corruption prosecutions, the two men who led that unit, also resigned."

This was followed by a report, from a separate journalist, to the effect that: "At least three more DOJ, Public Integrity Unit, senior officials resigned, after meeting the same top Justice Department official, on the Eric Adams case. Five in Public Integrity overall. That is six officials who have resigned…"!

This is referred to as "passive resistance", and is most commendable. These highly trained professionals took a stand, *on principle! They sacrificed their careers,* rather than compromise their principles. Bravo! If only I could meet them in person, and shake their hands!

That being said, I have no doubt that there are a great many other officials, who feel the same way. They have taken an oath to "preserve, protect and defend the Constitution", and that is precisely what they are doing. If that involves disobeying an illegal order, from a superior, then so be it!

Truly, the revolutionary movement is now very broad and deep. Trump and Musk may not realize it yet, but their days are numbered.

Gerald McIsaac

CHAPTER 16

Spiritual Power

It is a fundamental tenet of Marxism, that the state apparatus came into existence, at the same time that classes came into existence. Of course, those first classes were composed of slaves, and slave owners. As the slaves had a rather "annoying" habit of rebelling, the slave owners created an organization, a "state apparatus", whose sole purpose was to "discourage" such behaviour.

This generally involved men, frequently mounted on horseback, armed with weapons such as spears, swords, whips and clubs. In addition, as a means of discouraging any further "acts of insurrection", a method of execution was devised, which was as prolonged and painful, as possible. This was meant, not so much as punishment for rebelling, but to serve as a warning, to all other slaves. They were made aware that there was a heavy price to be paid, for rebellion.

The Romans perfected this method with the art of crucifixion, in which an individual could be nailed to a tree, and suffer a prolonged, painful death, for as long as a week.

Since that time, various classes have come into existence. The state apparatus has evolved, as the classes have evolved. It is now more subtle, less barbaric, but is still used by the ruling class, as a means of crushing the "lower classes".

It was Engels who conducted a detailed analysis of society, and published his conclusions, in his landmark work, The Origin of the Family, Private Property and the State. Concerning the state, Engels wrote: "The state is therefore by no means a power imposed on society from the outside; just as little is it 'the reality of the moral idea,' 'the image and reality of reason', as Hegel asserts. Rather, it is a product of society at a certain stage of development; it is the admission that this society has become entangled in an insoluble contradiction with itself, that it is cleft into irreconcilable antagonisms, which it is powerless to dispel. But in order that these antagonisms, classes with conflicting economic interests, might not consume themselves and society in sterile struggle, a power apparently standing above society became necessary, for the purpose of moderating the conflict and keeping it within the bounds of 'order'; and this power, arising out of society, but placing itself above it, and increasingly alienating itself from it, is the state."

It was Lenin, who also made clear his attitude to the state, in his great work, State and Revolution. As he stated: "The state is the product and the manifestation of the *irreconcilability* of class antagonisms. The state arises when, where and to the extent that class antagonisms *cannot* be objectively reconciled. And, conversely, the existence of the state proves that the class antagonisms *are* irreconcilable. (italics by Lenin)

In State and Revolution, Lenin stresses the necessity of *smashing* the existing state apparatus, which has been set up by the capitalists, for the sole purpose of crushing the working class. It must be replaced with a different state apparatus, for the purpose of crushing the monopoly capitalists, the multi billionaires, the bourgeoisie, as they make every effort, after the revolution, to "restore their paradise lost", to return to power. This new state apparatus, is referred to as the Dictatorship of the Proletariat.

That is quite well known, at least among Leftist people, especially Marxists, Communists. That which is not so well known, is that Lenin was referring to something more than the "physical force elements of repression". These physical forces include the police, military, jails, prisons and courts. As they are *visible*, it is relatively easy to target them! And rest assured, at the time of the Insurrection, they will be targeted and destroyed.

This brings me to the spiritual forces, which are also part of the bourgeois state apparatus, also used to crush the working class. As they are not visible, they are, all too often, at the time of the Revolution, overlooked. A huge mistake!

In the case of the *formerly* socialist Soviet Union, as well as the *formerly* socialist country of China, the capitalists were able to return to power, at least partly due to the fact that the spiritual power of the bourgeois, was not smashed.

As for those who are skeptical, concerning the existence of "spiritual power", may I refer you to that which Marx said, concerning the first working class attempt at self government, the Paris Commune:

"Having once got rid of the standing army and the police, the physical force elements of the old government, the Commune was anxious to break the *spiritual force* of repression, the 'parson power'". (my italics)

Allow me to add that there are various sources of spiritual power. That of the clergy, Marx referred to as "parson power". That of the scientists, academics and intellectuals, I refer to as "professor power". That professor power, the spiritual power of the bourgeois, was *not* smashed, in the Soviet Union, or in China.

Yet spiritual power is every bit as real, as the physical elements. Also invisible, which makes it more dangerous, in my opinion. The American bourgeois is supremely well aware of this, and has mastered the art of spiritual power, through their use of propaganda. It is a master piece of distortions, half truths, lies and deception. American propaganda sets the standard for bourgeois ideology!

For the benefit of those who are skeptical, allow me to provide one simple example. Most Americans are aware that slavery was abolished, by President Abraham Lincoln, with his historic Emancipation Proclamation, of January 1, 1863. The Great Emancipator! The pride of the Republican Party! His statue is displayed in Washington. Countless people visit that statue, every year, to honour his memory.

Reality check! Every fifth grader is well aware that the president does *not* have the authority to amend the Constitution. They are also well aware that, in 1857, the Supreme Court ruled, in the Dred Scott case, that slavery was guaranteed, in the Constitution. To abolish slavery required an Amendment to the Constitution, which is completely beyond the authority of the president.

Yet to this day, people continue to believe that Lincoln abolished slavery! Even those who know better, or *should know better, continue to believe this lie!* The spiritual power of bourgeois propaganda!

The sad fact is that very few Americans have even bothered to read that Proclamation. Even middle class, intellectual Americans, tend to believe those lies! Including those who consider themselves to be "Independent Socialists"!

Allow me to stress the fact that the Emancipation Proclamation is *not* called the Abolition Proclamation, for a reason. The word abolish is *not* mentioned, in that Proclamation!

The only slaves Lincoln "emancipated", were those over whom he had no control! Those were the slaves who were under the control of the Confederates! Those slaves were not released from bondage!

The slaves over whom he had control, those who were owned by slave owners, within the "slave states" which remained loyal to the Union, Lincoln *did not emancipate!*

Slavery was abolished in December, of 1865, almost three years after that famous Proclamation. By an Act of Congress, as required by Constitutional law.

There is a reason that I have gone into this, in such detail. Certainly not to offend any American middle class intellectuals! Especially not Independent Socialists! I consider such people to be my Brothers and Sisters, my Comrades In Arms! And very soon, they will be! Whether they know it or not, and they probably do not!

Some things just have to be said! Regardless of the consequences! Certain facts have to be faced! No matter how unpleasant those fact may be! One of those unpleasant facts, is that countless people, including middle class intellectuals, are under the influence of the spiritual power of the bourgeois! And most of them, are not even aware of this!

I can only hope that this will serve as a "wake up call". In that case, feel free to break those "invisible chains", the spiritual power of the bourgeois. Further face the fact that Marx and Lenin were correct. Social Scientists! Embrace those revolutionary theories! Take part in overthrowing the monopoly capitalists! The Oligarchy! Put Trump and Musk in their place! Under the Dictatorship of the Proletariat!

The alternative is a Dictatorship of the Oligarchy, led by Elon Musk.

Gerald McIsaac

CHAPTER 17

Celebrity Power

In my previous article, I documented the existence of spiritual power. This is every bit as real as the "physical force elements of repression", which the monopoly capitalists use, in order to crush the "lower classes". As this power is not visible, it is commonly overlooked, if not denied. It is high time we changed that! One good turn deserves another!

The bourgeois have been using spiritual power, against the working people, for many years. With great success, I might add. They are masters of the art of lies and deception. It is their belief, that if the lie is big enough, and repeated often enough, then "everyone" will believe it. This includes those who should know better!

As the astute reader may have already guessed, that previous statement was a none too subtle jab at all middle class intellectuals, including those who consider themselves to be Independent Socialists.

It is reasonable to assume that all such middle class intellectuals, have considerable academic training, including University degrees. As that is the case, they have no doubt been exposed to the Scientific Socialist theories of Marx and Lenin, as it is only in University that those theories are even mentioned.

I use the word "mentioned", and not "taught", as in University, it is only the bourgeois *distortion* of those scientific theories, that is taught. *Not* the true Scientific Socialist theories, of those two great Social Scientists!

The bourgeois would have us believe that society develops haphazardly, devoid of rhyme or reason! They think that we are blessed with capitalism, purely by chance, an "Act of God", and should be grateful, counting our blessings. The "Good Lord" has seen fit to send multi billionaires, the Oligarchy, to rule over us! They have the "Divine Right To Rule"! Nonsense!

On the contrary, society develops according to certain laws. It was Marx who first determined these laws, so perhaps it is best to let him explain them, in his own words, as he stated in 1852:

"And now as to myself, no credit is due to me for discovering the existence of classes in modern society, nor yet the struggle between them. Long before me, bourgeois historians had described the historical development of this class struggle, and bourgeois economists the economic anatomy of the classes. What I did that was new was to prove: 1) that the *existence of classes* is only bound up with *particular historical phases in the development of production;* 2) that the class struggle necessarily leads to the *Dictatorship of the Proletariat;* 3) that this Dictatorship itself only constitutes the transition to the *abolition of all classes and to a classless society."*

With regards to his first point, which is that "the existence of classes is only bound up with *particular historical phases in the development of production"*, bear in mind that it was the industrial revolution, as the "development of production", which gave birth to two new classes, the capitalist class, bourgeoisie, and the working class, proletariat. Those are now the two main classes in society!

As to the second point Marx made, which is that "the class struggle necessarily leads to the Dictatorship of the Proletariat", the key word here is "necessarily". As capitalism develops, the bourgeois becomes ever more powerful, and gradually succeeds in wiping out all other classes, aside from the proletariat. The bourgeois cannot exist without the proletariat! Yet their class interests are diametrically opposed. That which is in the best interests of the bourgeois, is in the worst interests of the proletariat. This is referred to as "class struggle". This class struggle will "necessarily lead" to Revolution, and the subsequent "Dictatorship of the Proletariat". This "Dictatorship" is necessary to crush the bourgeois, as after the revolution, they will make every effort to return to power, to "restore their paradise lost". This new "Dictatorship" will be exercised by the whole of the working class, the proletariat. Which is the reason it is called the Dictatorship of the Proletariat.

Concerning his third point, "that this Dictatorship (of the Proletariat) itself only constitutes the transition to the abolition of all classes and to a classless society". *After* the revolution, *after* the proletariat smashes the existing state apparatus, which has been set up, by the capitalists, in order to crush the "lower classes", *after* a new state apparatus is established, in the form of the Dictatorship of the Proletariat, in order to crush the bourgeois, then classes will gradually cease to exist, as all people learn to live and work together, for the common good, providing for the sick and needy. A true classless society.

This brings me to the subject of the Independent Socialists, many of whom are members of the Democratic Socialists of America, DSA. There are possibly ninety thousand members. Their website in on the internet, including their Political Platform, which contains a lengthy list of demands.

May I suggest that the multi billionaires, the Oligarchy, is not about to agree to any small part of those demands. Probably none whatsoever. After all, they are focused on establishing a Dictatorship, possibly a fascist state.

May I further suggest that the Oligarchy has to be stopped. This is going to require something more than the publication of a "wish list". It is going to require putting into practice the Scientific Socialist theories of Marx and Lenin.

I can only hope that no Independent Socialist, whether a member of DSA or not, takes offence to these remarks, although I am sure that many will do just that. Yet now is not the time for diplomacy. Certain things just have to be said, regardless of the consequences.

Ideally, many middle class, intellectual, Independent Socialists, whether members of DSA or not, will consider becoming Scientific Socialists. Face the fact that Marx and Lenin were correct. At the bare minimum, read State and Revolution, by Lenin. The Insurrection, which will kick off the Revolution, could start at any time. The Oligarchy is forcing the Revolution.

It is also very likely that a great many celebrities are Independent Socialists, or at least, have a favourable attitude towards socialism. Strangely enough, those individuals have a certain spiritual power. Especially those who are referred to as "Hollywood Movie Stars". By all means, use that power! Now is not the time to be shy! No false modesty! Your fans pay strict attention to whatever you say! That includes any political statements!

It is encouraging that there are a great many videos, on the internet, containing celebrities who are voicing their opposition, even their hatred, towards Trump and Musk. That is a step in the right direction.

Yet something more is required. Working people have to be exposed to class content. They have to be made aware of themselves, as a class, with their own class interests. Also made aware of the fact that the monopoly capitalists, the multi billionaires, the bourgeoisie, the Oligarchy, are our class enemies. What is more, this should be done in an entertaining manner. Education through entertainment!

These professional entertainers are the experts, in that department. The little exposure they have received, contains too little class content, and too much vulgarity. That merely detracts from the message.

The working people have to become aware that a Revolution is required, to overthrow the multi billionaires, the Oligarchy. There is no other way of preventing them from establishing a Dictatorship, possibly even a state of fascism. They must be overthrown, the existing state apparatus smashed, and then they must be crushed, under the Dictatorship of the Proletariat.

To express this, in an entertaining manner, is a tall order, but I have great faith in the Hollywood Celebrities. No doubt, they will rise to the occasion. I have complete confidence in them.

Gerald McIsaac

CHAPTER 18

Project 2025 Going Into Effect

As I write this, it is now late February, and true to his word, Trump has wasted no time in implementing his completely reactionary agenda, that of Project 2025. He is being assisted in this less than noble objective, by his "Lord and Master", Elon Musk. It is Musk who pulls the strings, and Trump "dances to his tune". It is safe to say that Trump is the finest Stooge, since Curly Howard!

The federal agencies in Washington, continue to be devastated by the "Trump-Musk purges". The military has been hard hit lately, with the firings of the Chairman of the Joint Chiefs of Staff, along with several other high ranking generals, as well as all three JAG commanders.

JAG stands for Judge Advocate General, and they are the "top lawyers" for the Army, Navy and Air Force. Their main duty is to advise the military officials, concerning the legalities of "military actions". As far as Trump is concerned, it is really quite simple: If he gives the order, it is legal, and must be carried out!

Yet the opposition to the "Trump-Musk coalition", as well as the "Oligarchy", is growing, becoming stronger daily. The working people are looking for leaders, and Bernie Sanders, the "Independent Senator from Vermont", the self described "Independent Socialist", is "rising to the occasion".

In an address to Congress, posted on the internet, under the title, "No God Kings Will Rule In America", Sanders gave a remarkable speech. As it is so important, I have chosen to reproduce it here:

"Future generations will look back at this moment, what we do right now, and remember whether we had the courage to defend our democracy, against the growing threats of Oligarchy, and authoritarianism. Elon Musk, the wealthiest man on the planet, is attempting to dismantle major agencies of the federal government, which are designed to protect the needs of working families and the disadvantaged.

"These agencies were created by the US Congress. and it is Congress's responsibility to maintain them, to reform them, or to end them. It is not Mr. Musk's responsibility. They will remember whether we stood with President Abraham Lincoln, at Gettysburg, who in 1863, looking out over a battle field where thousands of people had died…in the fight against slavery, and he stated that, 'this nation under God, shall have a new birth of freedom, and that a government of the people, by the people, for the people, shall not perish from the earth'.

"Do we stand with Lincoln's vision of America, or do we sit idly by and allow this country to move into a new vision, and that is a government of the billionaire class, by the billionaire class, for the billionaire class…

"But it is not just Oligarchy that we should be concerned about. Not just the reality that today, three people own more wealth than the bottom half of American society. A hundred and seventy million. Three people have more wealth than the bottom 170 million. It is not just that the gap between the very very rich and everyone else is growing wider ….more income and wealth inequity today than we have ever had …We are moving under Trump towards authoritarianism. More and more power resting in fewer and fewer hands…

"Elon Musk, the wealthiest man on the planet, is attempting to dismantle major agencies, of the federal government, which are designed to protect the needs of working families and the disadvantaged. These agencies were created by the US Congress, and it is Congress's responsibility to maintain them, to reform them or to end them. It is not Mr. Musk's responsibility. What Mr. Musk is doing is patently illegal, and Unconstitutional and must be ended. …

"President Trump attempted to suspend all federal grants and loans, an outrageous and clearly Unconstitutional act… under the Constitution…the

President can recommend legislation, he can support legislation, he can veto legislation, but he does not have the power to unilaterally terminate funding passed by the Congress…

"It is Congress, the House and the Senate, who control the purse strings, but in this move towards authoritarianism, it is not just the Congress that is being attacked, it is our judiciary…

"The Vice President…. said that 'judges are not allowed to control the executives legitimate power'. …One of the major functions of the federal courts, is to interpret our Constitution, and when appropriate, serve as a check on the Unconstitutional power of the executive. …

"Mr. Musk meanwhile, has proposed, 'that the worst one percent of appointed judges, be fired every year', and he demanded the impeachment of judges that have blocked him from accessing sensitive Treasury Department files. No doubt, under Mr Musk's rule, it will be him and his billionaire friends who determine who the worst judges are….you do not impeach judges who rule against you here in the US…

"Under the Constitution, we have a separation of powers, brilliantly crafted by the founding fathers of this country, in the 1770's….an executive branch, a legislative branch, and a judiciary …Mr. Trump and his friends are not just trying to undermine two of the three pillars of our Constitutional government, the Congress and the courts, they are also going after the media. …cannot have a functioning democracy, …without an independent press. …"

(This was followed by a list of major media news outlets which Trump has recently sued, using the power of his presidential office)

"The President, using his incredible power and the power of his agencies, to go after media in this country, who are saying and doing things he doesn't like. …Time to ask a simple question….What do Mr Trump and Mr Musk and their fellow billionaires, really want? …their endgame? their goal?…It is exactly what ruling classes through out history, have always wanted, and have always believed to be their right ..more power for themselves, more control for themselves, more wealth …they are determined to not allow democracy, and the rule of law to get in their way …the needs, the concerns, the pain, the ideas, the dreams, of ordinary people are simply an impediment, to what they the Oligarchs are entitled to. They actually believe this!"

(Sanders then went on to explain that, before the American Revolution of 1776, the ruling class of British nobility, believed that they had the "divine right of kings, appointed by God, not to be questioned by mere mortals")

"Now we have an ideology…that a very wealthy group of people …their absolute right to rule …Oligarchs of today are our modern day kings … their greed has no end"

(Sanders then listed the three richest men in the country, each of whom is worth several hundred billion dollars. It is clearly his opinion that these three multi billionaires form that which he refers to as the "Oligarchy". He also maintains that their wealth is equivalent to the "bottom half of American society, that of one hundred seventy million people". He went on to state that their wealth has soared dramatically, since the November election of Trump)

"Meanwhile, 60 percent of Americans live paycheck to paycheck, 85 Million are uninsured for medical, 25 percent of seniors are trying to survive on 15 thousand a year or less, 800 thousand are homeless, and we have the highest rate of childhood poverty of almost any major country on earth, and real inflation adjusted wages for the average American worker has not gone up in fifty years."

In my opinion, Sanders has "hit the nail right on the head"! He has provided us with a detailed, accurate description of the current situation in America. It is not a pretty sight!

As a result of this rather "grim situation", a "mass movement" has taken place, or a "grass roots, popular uprising", to phrase it in popular terms. The people taking part in this movement, are looking to Sanders for leadership. They want him to tell them what to do. This is documented quite well, in a video titled, "Massive Crowds Show Up For Bernie Sanders In Trump States".

At the start of the video, the narrator points out that a great many Americans are feeling "aimless", somewhat "frustrated with the Trump administration", and the "Democratic Party is not doing a whole lot to fight back against it".

That is putting it most politely! In fact, the Democratic Party is clearly "in cahoots" with the Republican Party! Both Parties serve the same class of monopoly capitalists, the multi billionaires, the bourgeoisie. As the class of monopoly capitalists has determined to change their method of rule, from that of a democratic republic, to that of an Oligarchy, both mainstream political parties have determined to submit, to the will of their political masters. This despite the fact that the Oligarchy plans to *abolish* both mainstream political parties! Both Republican and Democratic Parties, are now "falling on their swords"! Sacrificing themselves, out of love for the monopoly capitalists!

The narrator then went on to point out the fact that there is no election campaign, yet a great many people are showing up, for the Sanders "Fight the Oligarchy Tour". As Sanders phrases it, on his posters, "Together we must say NO to oligarchy, NO to authoritarianism, NO to massive cuts in Medicaid and NO to huge tax breaks to billionaires".

An excellent idea! But just how do we achieve those most noble objectives?

As Sanders stated, in one of his town hall meetings, "Trumpism will not be defeated by politicians inside the DC Beltway. That is not going to happen. It will be defeated by millions of Americans ….all over this country, who come together, at a grass roots level…in a movement that says no to Oligarchy, no to authoritarianism, no to kleptocracy, no massive cuts to programs, that the working class desperately needs, and no to huge tax breaks for the billionaires and the one percent."

Sanders certainly has a point there! He sounds very much like a Scientific Socialist! A true Marxist! A Communist! Yet with his next statement, he reverted to his true, middle class, Utopian Socialism, nature.

The course of action, recommended by Sanders? That the voters, within Congressional Districts controlled by Republican Members of Congress, apply pressure, to their Member of Congress, to *vote against these tax breaks!*

As if that is about to do a world of good! Both mainstream political parties have resigned themselves to their fate, to that of being abolished, as the Oligarchy takes power. So no Member of Congress can be threatened with removal from office, as that office is about to be abolished! An empty threat!

Senator Bernie Sanders is a very intelligent man. He is a highly respected leader of the working people, a Member of the Democratic Socialists of America, DSA, and well aware of the plan, of the Oligarchs, to abolish the democratic republic. As he stated, the Oligarchs are not about to "allow the rule of law to get in their way". He even compared them to the monarchs of yesteryear, including the British nobility, which formerly ruled the American colonies. Absolutely correct!

Yet in order to stop the Oligarchy, Sanders is suggesting a strictly legal, non violent course of action. As if that is about to impress the Oligarchy! As far as they are concerned, laws are made to be broken!

The proper approach, is to combine legal and illegal action, while not ruling out violence. As well as the legal action, recommended by Sanders, may I suggest a legal challenge to the 2024 Presidential election, on the grounds that it was Unconstitutional, in direct violation of the Twelfth Amendment. A Supreme Court ruling, to that effect, would remove both Trump and Vance from office.

At the same time, on the "illegal front", so to speak, preparations must be intensified, for the approaching Insurrection. The Oligarchy is determined to seize power, is in the process of seizing power, with no regard for legalities, as they think that they have the "divine right to rule"! A mere Supreme Court decision is not about to impress them!

With that in mind, may I suggest further training, arming and equipping of Councils, as I have outlined in previous articles. In secret, of course, as far as possible. Part of that training may involve the study of the key works of Marxism, such as the Communist Manifesto, State and Revolution, Imperialism, the Highest Stage of Capitalism, What Is To Be Done?, and Left Wing Communism, An Infantile Disorder.

In conclusion, we can say that the monopoly capitalists, the multi billionaires, the bourgeoisie, have decided to change their method of rule, from that of a democratic republic, to a straight forward dictatorship, in the form of an Oligarchy. This involves abolishing the legislative and judicial branches of government, which is to say, both the Senate and House of Representatives, as well as all courts. Further, both mainstream political parties have agreed to this. They are surrendering their power to the Oligarchy.

The common people, by whom I mean the workers and family farmers, must be made aware of this. They must be encouraged to become politically active, as experience is such a fine teacher. Take the advice of Sanders, all of which is perfectly legal, and see what happens. No change!

At the same time, consider the revolutionary works of Marx and Lenin. These are readily available on the internet, even in audio form. This is to drive home the fact that the existing state apparatus must be *smashed,* at the time of the Insurrection, and replaced with a new state apparatus, in the form of the Dictatorship of the Proletariat, in order to crush the multi billionaires. Rest assured, after the successful socialist revolution, they will make every effort to return to power.

The future lies with Scientific Socialism, in the form of Councils, exercising power through the Dictatorship of the Proletariat. Now the common people have to be made aware of this.

Gerald McIsaac

CHAPTER 19

Concerning Allegations That Trump Is A Russian Asset

There are several videos available, on the internet, alleging that Trump is a "Russian Asset". These are very serious allegations, as Trump is not only the American head of state, but also the Commander In Chief of all branches of the military. To accuse him of being in the service of a foreign government, is to accuse him of High Treason, a capital offence.

Yet strangely, Trump has not responded to any of these allegations. This is most surprising, as there is a heavy financial penalty to be paid for slander. Trump can personally testify to that! He has successfully sued several media outlets, quite recently. As well, he has been on the receiving end of such lawsuits. Yet he has refused to file a lawsuit against any of the people, making those allegations!

Incidentally, the legal definition of slander is that a statement is false, and maliciously made. Naturally, as long as indisputable proof exists, that the statement is true, there can be no question of slander. Could it be that Trump is not suing for slander, because there is no slander?

These most serious allegations, that of High Treason, on the part of Donald Trump, are being made by a former high ranking KGB agent, by the name of Alnur Mussayev. This gentleman claims, in a Facebook post, that "Trump was recruited by the KGB in 1987". He further alleges that Trump was given the code name of "Krasnov". He went on to say that "Trumps narcissism made him an ideal target for recruitment by Moscow". What is more, he also alleges that "Trumps personal KGB file is still active and is managed by Putin's close allies". He goes on to state that the current policies, of the Trump administration, are explained by these facts.

Incidentally, for the benefit of those readers who are not experts in psychology, I should mention that the definition of a narcissist is that of someone who "has an unreasonably high opinion of themselves, need and seek too much attention and want people to admire them. They also do not understand, or care, about the feelings of others". That is a near perfect description of Donald Trump!

I can further add, that the KGB is the Russian equivalent of the American CIA. The members of both spy agencies are well trained, highly skilled, professional liars. For that reason, anything they say is at best, questionable.

Those who support these allegations, against Trump, point to the "2017 Steele Dossier", which also cites "compromising material" against Trump. Yet critics point out, correctly, that the Dossier contains references to "anonymous sources", so cannot be trusted. After all, such sources are little better than rumours.

This brings us to a second former KGB agent, Yori Shvets, who also alleges that Trump was recruited by the KGB, as a "Russian Asset", in his 2021 book. He claims that Russian interest in Trump began even earlier, in the "late seventies", due to Trump's real estate business. His marriage, in 1977, to Ivana Zelnickova, a beautiful Czech model, first brought him to the attention of the Czech Intelligence. Shvets goes on to say that "Trump's 1987 trip to Moscow marked a key moment in his alleged recruitment".

There are further allegations, on the internet, that "In 2008, Russian oligarch Dmitry Rybolovlev also helped Trump, during a debt crisis, by buying his Palm Beach property". Of course, Trump most emphatically denies all of these allegations.

Another individual, by the name of Sacha Sotnik, has recently made two videos, posted on the internet. He describes himself as a "former high ranking member of the USSR, one who had access to top secret information". He maintains that he is now an "independent journalist, living and working in Slovakia".

One of those videos is titled, "Trump is a KGB agent", while the other is titled, "Impeachment or Treason?". He alleges that the KGB not only recruited Trump in 1978, but also "played a key role in his victory, in the 2024 election. This information may become the basis for impeachment, and even charges of treason."

Certainly, no one is his right mind, is about to take the word of any former member of the KGB, or of any Russian Oligarch, for that matter. So it is correct to be skeptical of these allegations, to put it politely. After all, such individuals are habitual liars.

The same cannot be said of the former Acting Director of the FBI, Andrew McCabe. If there is any American government official, current or former, whom we can trust, it is Andrew McCabe.

With that in mind, consider the fact that several years ago, during the first Trump administration, CNN conducted an interview with McCabe. This is covered in a video, currently posted on the internet, titled: "McCabe: It's possible that Trump is a Russian asset".

The headline of the video reads, "McCabe: From the very beginning, the president continuously undermined the Russia investigation; the question is why?"

One of the latest videos, making similar allegations, is that of Craig Unger. It is titled, "US author explains Donald Trump's Russia, KGB connections". The narrator says he has written two books on the subject. He claims to be "completely certain that Trump is a Russian asset". He also say that "not a single one of his facts has been challenged". One of these "facts" is that, as early as 1987, Trump called for pulling out of NATO, and aligning the US with Russia. Which is precisely what he is doing now. He also made a reference to an old movie, "The Manchurian Candidate", in which Russia manages to secure a "Communist" in the White House. Is it possible that life is imitating art?

I mention these videos, in order to stress the fact that these allegations are widespread, if nothing else. What is more, they are very likely to become ever more widespread. Especially after the February 28 meeting, between Trump and Zelensky, in the Oval Office, of the White House, in the presence of a great many journalists.

The full video is readily available, on the internet, and is being widely discussed. The journalists are agreed that the meeting "devolved into an Oval Office shouting match". They are also agreed that Trump just "stood American foreign policy on its head"!

This is to say that, for the last eighty years, since the end of the Second World War, "America has been at the centre of an alliance, with Western European countries, against the power of Russia". Not any more! Now America is aligned with Russia, against the countries of Western Europe! Now what could possibly have provoked such a dramatic shift in foreign policy? Could there be a particle of truth to the allegations that Trump is a Russian asset? One thing is clear: whether or not Trump is a Russian asset, Putin could not possibly be more pleased with him!

It has even been suggested that this could be grounds for impeachment, and subsequent removal from office. That is not about to happen! There is no chance of Trump being removed from office, as a result of impeachment proceedings. Even if Trump was to be removed from office, such a removal would not resolve the fundamental problem, that of stopping the Oligarchy, led by Elon Musk, from seizing power.

As I have documented in previous writings, that which is required is the application of legal and illegal measures. Such legal measures include the application of the Twelfth Amendment to the Constitution, so that the Supreme Court could rule that Trump is a fraudulent President, and Vance is a fraudulent Vice President.

That would not completely stop the threatened take over, by Elon Musk and the other members of the Oligarchy, but would certainly be a big step in the right direction. That requires the cooperation of the common people, workers and family farmers. Yet such a removal from office, may well inspire those people. At least, it would prove to the skeptical, that the Oligarchy can be beaten.

For the moment, may our signs and posters, as well as our emails, contain the following slogans:

Stop the Oligarchy!

Dictatorship of the Proletariat!

Workers of the World, Unite!

Scientific Socialism!

CHAPTER 20

Open Letter To American Workers

For a great many years, Canadians and Americans have been close friends and neighbours. Many Canadians and Americans are related. We share the largest unguarded border in the world. We frequently cross the border, for vacation and business. Or at least, that is the way it used to be. Not any more!

Very recently, President Donald Trump announced tariffs on goods produced in Canada, Mexico and China. A tariff is nothing other than a tax, placed on certain goods produced in another country, in this case Canada, and then sold in the United States. This added tax goes to the American government, but is paid by the American consumer.

As can be expected, Canada responded with tariffs of their own, referred to as "retaliatory tariffs", so that certain goods produced in America, to be sold in Canada, are also now taxed. Here again, the tax goes to the Canadian government, but is paid by the Canadian consumer. Then, as the two countries impose ever more retaliatory tariffs, on ever more products, this gives rise to that which is politely referred to as a "trade war".

It is more accurately referred to as simple stupidity! Madness! The consumers of both countries, are faced with ever higher prices. Inflation! The very thing that Trump swore that he would abolish!

Aside from inflation, tariffs play a key role, in monopoly capitalism. As Lenin explained, in Imperialism, the Highest Stage of Capitalism, in reference to tariffs:

"The concentration of industry and the formation of monopolist, manufacturers combines, cartels, syndicates, etc., could only be accelerated by these circumstances".

This is to stress the fact, that the use of tariffs, merely *"accelerates"* the development of monopoly capitalism! Yet, as we already live under a state of monopoly capitalism, it is safe to say that those tariffs merely strengthen the capitalist monopolies!

Compare this to the nonsense that Trump spits out, to the effect that, "tariffs will force American companies to produce goods, strictly for American consumers". Precisely the opposite is the case! The existing monopolies are about to become ever more powerful, ever more complete! Ever more small businesses are about to "bite the dust".

As well, Trump is determined to make Canada the "Fifty First State". He has even insulted our Prime Minister, Justin Trudeau, by referring to him as "Governor Trudeau". Make no mistake, Canadians are not taking this lying down!

We are all proud of our Prime Minister, for the speech he gave recently. It is on the internet, titled "Watch Trudeau Speak Directly To Trump During Blistering Speech".

He started his speech by pointing out that: "Today, the United States launched a trade war against Canada. Their closest partner and ally, their closest friend."

That is exactly right! And what close "partner and ally" is about to take the place of Canada?

"At the same time, they are talking about working positively with Russia, appeasing Vladimir Putin, a lying murderous dictator. ...Canadians are reasonable, and we are polite, but we will not back down from a fight. Not when our country and the well being of everyone in it is at stake."

Well spoken! He went on to state that Canada will respond with "retaliatory tariffs". This is to say that Canada will, in turn, place tariffs on certain goods produced in America, and sent to Canada, to be sold.

He was also correct when he stated that, "there are no winners in a trade war". Then he spoke directly to the American people:

"We do not want this. We want to work with you, as a friend and ally, and we do not want to see you hurt either. But your government has chosen to do this, to you. … Your government has chosen to put American jobs at risk, at the thousands of workplaces that succeed because of materials from Canada, or because of consumers in Canada, or both. …They have chosen to launch a trade war that will, first and foremost, harm American families".

It is significant that the "trade war", to which Trudeau is referring, is nothing other than the response of one country, in this case Canada, to the tariffs of another country, in this case America. What choice do we have?

Yet Americans are a heroic people, with a history of revolution, of which they can be most proud. No doubt, they will soon expand upon that revolutionary history, and crush Trump and the Oligarchy, those who are determined to destroy the American democratic republic.

In fact, Lenin wrote an open letter to all American workers, in 1918. As it is so important, I have chosen to reproduce it, in full, although perhaps a little explanation is in order.

The first true Russian Marxists referred to themselves as "Social Democrats", as they fought for democracy, as well as socialism. But then the Party split, into a majority, or Bolsheviks, those who adhere to principle, led by Lenin, and a minority, or Mensheviks, those who were completely unprincipled. Still later, the Bolsheviks referred to themselves as Communists.

The family farmers were referred to as peasants, and were divided into poor, middle and rich. The rich peasants were referred to as "kulaks", or "tight fists", or the "rural bourgeoisie". They were the class enemies of the poor peasants and the workers.

The word Soviet means "Council" in English, and these Councils have now made an appearance in America.

The expression "i.e." means "that is". Also, all italics were made by Lenin.

The following is the full content of the letter:

"Comrades! A Russian Bolshevik who took part in the 1905 Revolution, and who lived in your country for many years afterwards, has offered to convey my letter to you. I have accepted his proposal all the more gladly because just at the present time the American revolutionary workers have to play an exceptionally important role as uncompromising enemies of American imperialism—the freshest, strongest and latest in joining in the world-wide slaughter of nations for the division of capitalist profits. At this very moment, the American multimillionaires, these modern slaveowners have turned an exceptionally tragic page in the bloody history of bloody imperialism by giving their approval- whether direct or indirect, open or hypocritically concealed, makes no difference—to the armed expedition launched by the brutal Anglo-Japanese imperialists for the purpose of throttling the first socialist republic.

"The history of modern, civilized America opened with one of those great, really liberating, really revolutionary wars of which there have been so few compared to the vast number of wars of conquest which, like the present imperialist war, were caused by squabbles among kings, landowners or capitalists over the division of usurped land or ill gotten gains. That was the war the American people waged against the British robbers who oppressed America and held her in colonial slavery, in the same way as these "civilized" bloodsuckers are still oppressing and holding in colonial slavery hundreds of millions of people in India, Egypt, and all parts of the world.

"About 150 years have passed since then. Bourgeois civilization has borne all its luxurious fruits. America has taken first place among the free and educated nations in level of development of the productive forces of collective human endeavour, in the utilization of machinery and of all the wonders of modern engineering. At the same time, America has become one of the foremost countries in regard to the depth of the abyss which lies between the handful of arrogant multimillionaires who wallow in filth and luxury, and the millions of working people who constantly live on the verge of pauperism. The American people, who set the world an example in waging a revolutionary war against feudal slavery, now find themselves in the latest, capitalist stage of wage-slavery to a handful of multimillionaires, and find themselves playing the role of hired thugs who, for the benefit of wealthy scoundrels, throttled the Philippines in 1898 on the pretext of 'liberating' them, and are throttling the Russian Socialist Republic in 1918 on the pretext of 'protecting' it from the Germans.

"The four years of the imperialist slaughter of nations, however, have not passed in vain. The deception of the people by the scoundrels of both robber groups, the British and the German, has been utterly exposed by indisputable and obvious facts. The results of the four years of war have revealed the general law of capitalism as applied to war between robbers for the division of spoils: the richest and strongest profited and grabbed most, while the weakest were utterly robbed, tormented, crushed and strangled.

"The British imperialist robbers were the strongest in number of 'colonial slaves'. The British capitalists have not lost an inch of 'their territory (i.e., territory they have grabbed over the centuries), but they have grabbed all the German colonies in Africa, they have grabbed Mesopotamia and Palestine, they have throttled Greece, and have begun to plunder Russia.

"The German imperialist robbers were the strongest in organization and discipline of 'their' armies, but weaker in regard to colonies. They have lost all their colonies, but plundered half of Europe and throttled the largest number of small countries and weak nations. What a great war of 'liberation' on both sides! How well the robbers of both groups, the Anglo-French and the German capitalists, together with their lackeys, the social-chauvinists, i.e., the socialists who went over to the side of *their own* bourgeoisie, have 'defended their country'!

"The American multimillionaires were, perhaps, richest of all, and geographically the most secure. They have profited more than all the rest. They have converted all, even the richest, countries into their tributaries. They have grabbed hundreds of billions of dollars. And every dollar is sullied with filth: the filth of the secret treaties between Britain and her 'allies', between Germany and her vassals, treaties for the division of the spoils, treaties of mutual 'aid' for oppressing the workers and persecuting the internationalist socialists. Every dollar is sullied with the filth of 'profitable' war contracts, which in every country made the rich richer and the poor poorer. And every dollar is stained with blood—from that ocean of blood that has been shed by the ten million killed and twenty million maimed in the great, noble, liberating and holy war to decide whether the British or the German robbers are to get most of the spoils, whether the British or the German thugs are to be *foremost* in throttling the weak nations all over the world.

"While the German robbers broke all records in war atrocities, the British have broken all records not only in the number of colonies they have grabbed, but also in the subtlety of their disgusting hypocrisy. This very day, the Anglo-French and American bourgeois newspapers are spreading, in millions and millions of copies, lies and slander about Russia, and are hypocritically justifying their predatory expedition against her on the plea that they want to 'protect' Russia from the Germans!

"It does not require many words to refute this despicable and hideous lie; it is sufficient to point to one well-known fact. In October 1917, after the Russian workers had overthrown their imperialist government, the Soviet government, the government of the revolutionary workers and peasants, openly proposed a just peace, a peace without annexations or indemnities, a peace that fully guaranteed equal rights to all nations—and it proposed such a peace to *all* the belligerent countries.

"It was the Anglo-French and the American bourgeoisie who refused to accept our proposal; it was they who even refused to talk to us about a general peace! It was *they* who betrayed the interests of all nations; it was they who prolonged the imperialist slaughter!

"It was they who, banking on the possibility of dragging Russia back into the imperialist war, refused to take part in the peace negotiations and thereby gave a free hand to the no less predatory German capitalists who imposed the annexationist and harsh Brest Peace upon Russia!

"It is difficult to imagine anything more disgusting than the hypocrisy with which the Anglo-French and American bourgeoisie are now 'blaming us *for* the Brest Peace Treaty. The very capitalists of those countries which could have turned the Brest negotiations into general negotiations for a general peace are now our 'accusers'! The Anglo-French imperialist vultures, who have profited from the plunder of colonies and the slaughter of nations, have prolonged the war for nearly a whole year after Brest, and yet they 'accuse' *us,* the Bolsheviks, who proposed a just peace to all countries, they accuse *us,* who tore up, published and exposed to public disgrace the secret, criminal treaty concluded between the ex-tsar and the Anglo-French capitalists.

"The workers of the whole world, no matter in what country they live, greet us, sympathize with us, applaud us for breaking the iron ring of imperialist ties, of sordid imperialist treaties, of imperialist chains—for breaking through to freedom, and making the heaviest sacrifices in doing so—for, as a socialist republic, although torn and plundered by the imperialists, keeping *out* of the imperialist war and raising the banner of peace, the banner of socialism for the whole world to see.

"Small wonder that the international imperialist gang hates us for this, that it 'accuses' us, that all the lackeys of the imperialists, including our Right Socialist-Revolutionaries and Mensheviks, also 'accuse' us. The hatred these watchdogs of imperialism express for the Bolsheviks, and the sympathy of the class-conscious workers of the world, convince us more than ever of the justice of our cause.

"A real socialist would not fail to understand that for the sake of achieving victory over the bourgeoisie, for the sake of power passing to the workers, for the sake of *starting* the world proletarian revolution, we *cannot* and must *not* hesitate to make the heaviest sacrifices, including the sacrifice of part of our territory, the sacrifice of heavy defeats at the hands of imperialism. A real socialist would have proved by *deeds* his willingness for 'his' country to make the greatest sacrifice to give a real push forward to the cause of the socialist revolution.

"For the sake of 'their' cause, that is, for the sake of winning world hegemony, the imperialists of Britain and Germany have not hesitated to utterly ruin and throttle a whole number of countries, from Belgium and Serbia to Palestine and Mesopotamia. But must socialists wait with 'their' cause, the cause of liberating the working people of the whole world from the yoke of capital, of winning universal and lasting peace, until a path without sacrifice is found? Must they fear to open the battle until an easy victory is 'guaranteed'? Must they place the integrity and security of 'their' bourgeois-created 'fatherland' above the interests of the world socialist revolution? The scoundrels in the international socialist movement who think this way, those lackeys who grovel to bourgeois morality, thrice stand condemned.

"The Anglo-French and American imperialist vultures 'accuse' us of concluding an 'agreement' with German imperialism. What hypocrites, what scoundrels they are to slander the workers' government while trembling because of the sympathy displayed towards us by the workers of 'their own' countries! But their hypocrisy will be exposed. They pretend not to see the difference between an agreement entered into by 'socialists' with the bourgeoisie (their own or foreign) *against the workers,* against the working people, and an agreement entered into *for the protection* of the workers who have defeated their bourgeoisie, with the bourgeoisie of one national colour *against the bourgeoisie* of another colour in order that the proletariat may take advantage of the antagonisms between the different groups of bourgeoisie.

"In actual fact, every European sees this difference very well, and, as I shall show in a moment, the American people have had a particularly striking 'illustration' of it in their own history. There are agreements and agreements, there are *fagots et fagots,* as the French say.

"When in February 1918 the German imperialist vultures hurled their forces against unarmed, demobilized Russia, who had relied on the international solidarity of the proletariat before the world revolution had fully matured, I did not hesitate for a moment to enter into an 'agreement' with the French monarchists. Captain Sadoul, a French army officer who, in words, sympathized with the Bolsheviks, but was in deeds a loyal and faithful servant of French imperialism, brought the French officer de Lubersac to see me. 'I am a monarchist. My only aim is to secure the defeat of Germany,' de Lubersac declared to me. 'That goes without saying *(cela va sans dire)*, I replied. But this did not in the least prevent me from entering into an 'agreement' with de Lubersac concerning certain services that French army officers, experts in explosives, were ready to render us by blowing up railway lines in order to hinder the German invasion. This is an example of an 'agreement' of which every class-conscious worker will approve, an agreement in the interests of socialism. The French monarchist and I shook hands, although we knew that each of us would willingly hang his 'partner'. But for a time our interests coincided. Against the advancing rapacious Germans, *we,* in the interests of the Russian and the world socialist revolution, utilized the equally rapacious counter interests of *other* imperialists. In this way we served the interests of the working class of Russia and of other countries, we strengthened the proletariat and weakened the bourgeoisie of the whole world, we resorted to the methods, most legitimate and essential in *every* war, of manoeuvre, stratagem, retreat, in anticipation of the moment when the rapidly maturing proletarian revolution in a number of advanced countries *completely matured."*

"However much the Anglo-French and American imperialist sharks fume with rage, however much they slander us, no matter how many millions they spend on bribing the Right Socialist-Revolutionary, Menshevik and other social-patriotic newspapers, *I shall not hesitate one second* to enter into a *similar* 'agreement' with the German imperialist vultures if an attack upon Russia by Anglo-French troops calls for it. And I know perfectly well that my tactics will be approved by the class-conscious proletariat of Russia, Germany, France, Britain, America—in short, of the whole civilized world. Such tactics will ease the task of the socialist revolution, will hasten it, will weaken the international bourgeoisie, will strengthen the position of the working class which is defeating the bourgeoisie.

"The American people resorted to these tactics long ago to the advantage of their revolution. When they waged their great war of liberation against the British oppressors, they had also against them the French and the Spanish oppressors who owned a part of what is now the United States of North America. In their arduous war for freedom, the American people also entered into 'agreements' with some oppressors against others for the purpose of weakening the oppressors and strengthening those who were fighting in a revolutionary manner against oppression, for the purpose of serving the interests of the oppressed *people*. The American people took advantage of the strife between the French, the Spanish and the British; sometimes they even fought side by side with the forces of the French and Spanish oppressors against the British oppressors; first they defeated the British and then freed themselves (partly by ransom) from the French and the Spanish.

"Historical action is not the pavement of Nevsky Prospekt, said the great Russian revolutionary Chernyshevsky. A revolutionary would not 'agree' to a proletarian revolution only 'on the condition' that it proceeds easily and smoothly, that there is, from the outset, combined action on the part of the proletarians of different countries, that there are guarantees against defeats, that the road of the revolution is broad, free and straight, that it will not be necessary during the march to victory to sustain the heaviest casualties, to 'bide one's time in a besieged fortress', or to make one's way along extremely narrow, impassable, winding and dangerous mountain tracks. Such a person is no revolutionary, he has not freed himself from the pedantry of the bourgeois intellectuals; such a person will be found constantly slipping into the camp of the counter revolutionary bourgeoisie, like our Right Socialist-Revolutionaries, Mensheviks and even (although more rarely) Left Socialist-Revolutionaries.

"Echoing the bourgeoisie, these gentlemen like to blame us for the 'chaos' of the revolution, for the 'destruction' of industry, for the unemployment and the food shortage. How hypocritical these accusations are, coming from those who welcomed and supported the imperialist war, or who entered into an 'agreement' with Kerensky who continued this war! It is this imperialist war that is the cause of all these misfortunes. The revolution engendered by the war can not avoid the terrible difficulties and suffering bequeathed it by the prolonged, ruinous, reactionary slaughter of the nations. To blame us for the 'destruction' of industry, or for the 'terror', is either hypocrisy or dull-witted pedantry; it reveals an inability to understand the basic conditions of the fierce class struggle, raised to the highest degree of intensity that is called revolution.

"Even when 'accusers' of this type do 'recognize' the class struggle, they limit themselves to verbal recognition; actually, they constantly slip into the philistine utopia of class 'agreement' and 'collaboration'; for in revolutionary epochs the class struggle has always, inevitably, and in every country, assumed the form of *civil war,* and civil war is inconceivable without the severest destruction, terror and the restriction of formal democracy in the interests of this war. Only unctuous parsons—whether Christian or 'secular' in the persons of parlour, parliamentary socialists— cannot see, understand and feel this necessity. Only a life less 'man in the muffler' can shun the revolution for this reason instead of plunging into battle with the utmost ardour and determination at a time when history demands that the greatest problems of humanity be solved by struggle and war.

"The American people have a revolutionary tradition which has been adopted by the best representatives of the American proletariat, who have repeatedly expressed their complete solidarity with us Bolsheviks. That tradition is the war of liberation against the British in the eighteenth century and the Civil War in the nineteenth century. In some respects, if we only take into consideration the 'destruction' of some branches of industry and of the national economy, America in 1870 was behind 1860. But what a pedant, what an idiot would anyone be to deny on these grounds the immense, world-historic, progressive and revolutionary significance of the American Civil War of 1863-65!

"The representatives of the bourgeoisie understand that for the sake of overthrowing Negro slavery, of overthrowing the rule of the slaveowners, it was worth letting the country go through long years of civil war, through the abysmal ruin, destruction and terror that accompany every war. But now, when we are confronted with the vastly greater task of overthrowing capitalist *wage*-slavery, of overthrowing the rule of the bourgeoisie—now, the representatives and defenders of the bourgeoisie, and also the reformist socialists who have been frightened by the bourgeoisie and are shunning the revolution, cannot and do not want to understand that civil war is necessary and legitimate.

"The American workers will not follow the bourgeoisie. They will be with us, for civil war against the bourgeoisie. The whole history of the world and of the American labour movement strengthens my conviction that this is so. I also recall the words of one of the most beloved leaders of the American proletariat, Eugene Debs, who wrote in the *Appeal to Reason,* I believe towards the end of 1915, in the article "What Shall I Fight For" (I quoted this article at the beginning of 1916 at a public meeting of workers in Berne, Switzerland)—that he, Debs, would rather be shot than vote credits for the present criminal and reactionary war; that he, Debs, knows of only one holy and, from the proletarian standpoint, legitimate war, namely: the war against the capitalists, the war to liberate mankind from wage-slavery.

"I am not surprised that Wilson, the head of the American multimillionaires and servant of the capitalist sharks, has thrown Debs into prison. Let the bourgeoisie be brutal to the true internationalists, to the true representatives of the revolutionary proletariat! The more fierce and brutal they are, the nearer the day of the victorious proletarian revolution.

"We are blamed for the destruction caused by our revolution. . . . Who are the accusers? The hangers-on of the bourgeoisie, of that very bourgeoisie who, during the four years of the imperialist war, have destroyed almost the whole of European culture and have reduced Europe to barbarism, brutality and starvation. These bourgeoisie now demand we should not make a revolution on these ruins, amidst this wreckage of culture, amidst the wreckage and ruins created by the war, nor with the people who have been brutalized by the war. How humane and righteous the bourgeoisie are!

"Their servants accuse us of resorting to terror. . . . The British bourgeoisie have forgotten their 1649, the French bourgeoisie have forgotten their 1793. Terror was just and legitimate when the bourgeoisie resorted to it for their own benefit against feudalism. Terror became monstrous and criminal when the workers and poor peasants dared to use it against the bourgeoisie! Terror was just and legitimate when used for the purpose of substituting one exploiting minority for another exploiting minority. Terror became monstrous and criminal when it began to be used for the purpose of overthrowing *every* exploiting minority, to be used in the interests of the vast actual majority, in the interests of the proletariat and semi-proletariat, the working class and the poor peasants!

"The international imperialist bourgeoisie have slaughtered ten million men and maimed twenty million in 'their' war, the war to decide whether the British or the German vultures are to rule the world.

"If *our* war, the war of the oppressed and exploited against the oppressors and the exploiters, results in half a million or a million casualties in all countries, the bourgeoisie will say that the former casualties are justified, while the latter are criminal.

"The proletariat will have something entirely different to say.

"Now, amidst the horrors of the imperialist war, the proletariat is receiving a most vivid and striking illustration of the great truth taught by all revolutions and bequeathed to the workers by their best teachers, the founders of modern socialism. This truth is that no revolution can be successful unless *the resistance of the exploiters is crushed*. When we, the workers and toiling peasants, captured state power, it became our duty to crush the resistance of the exploiters. We are proud we have been doing this. We regret we are not doing it with sufficient firmness and determination.

"We know that fierce resistance to the socialist revolution on the part of the bourgeoisie is inevitable in all countries, and that this resistance will *grow* with the growth of this revolution. The proletariat will crush this resistance; during the struggle against the resisting bourgeoisie it will finally mature for victory and for power.

"Let the corrupt bourgeois press shout to the whole world about every mistake our revolution makes. We are not daunted by our mistakes. People have not become saints because the revolution has begun. The toiling classes who for centuries have been oppressed, downtrodden and forcibly held in the vice of poverty, brutality and ignorance cannot avoid mistakes when making a revolution. And, as I pointed out once before, the corpse of bourgeois society cannot be nailed in a coffin and buried. The corpse of capitalism is decaying and disintegrating in our midst, polluting the air and poisoning our lives, enmeshing that which is new, fresh, young and virile in thousands of threads and bonds of that which is old, moribund and decaying.

"For every hundred mistakes we commit, and which the bourgeoisie and their lackeys (including our own Mensheviks and Right Socialist-Revolutionaries) shout about to the whole world, 10,000 great and heroic deeds are performed, greater and more heroic because they are simple and inconspicuous amidst the everyday life of a factory district or a remote village, performed by people who are not accustomed (and have no opportunity) to shout to the whole world about their successes.

"But even if the contrary were true—although I know such an assumption is wrong—even if we committed 10,000 mistake for every 100 correct actions we performed, even in that case our revolution would be great and invincible, and *so it will be in the eyes of world history,* because, *for the first time,* not the minority, not the rich alone, not the educated alone, but the real people, the vast majority of the working people, are *themselves* building a new life, are *by their own experience* solving the most difficult problems of socialist organization .

"Every mistake committed in the course of such work, in the course of this most conscientious and earnest work of tens of millions of simple workers and peasants in reorganizing their whole life, every such mistake is worth thousands and millions of "lawless" successes achieved by the exploiting minority—successes in swindling and duping the working people. For only *through* such mistakes will the workers and peasants *learn* to build the new life, learn to do *without* capitalists; only in this way will they hack a path for themselves—through thousands of obstacles—to victorious socialism.

"Mistakes are being committed in the course of their revolutionary work by our peasants, who at one stroke, in one night, October 25-26 (old style), 1917, entirely abolished the private ownership of land, and are now, month after month, overcoming tremendous difficulties and correcting their mistakes themselves, solving in a practical way the most difficult tasks of organizing new conditions of economic life, of fighting the kulaks, providing land for the *working people* (and not for the rich), and of changing to *communist* large-scale agriculture.

"Mistakes are being committed in the course of their revolutionary work by our workers, who have already, after a few months, nationalized almost all the biggest factories and plants, and are learning by hard, everyday work the new task of managing whole branches of industry, are setting the nationalized enterprises going, overcoming the powerful resistance of inertia, petty-bourgeois mentality and selfishness, and, brick by brick, are laying the foundation of *new* social ties, of a *new* labour discipline, of a *new* influence of the workers' trade unions over their members.

"Mistakes are committed in the course of their revolutionary work by our Soviets, which were created as far back as 1905 by a mighty upsurge of the people. The Soviets of Workers and Peasants are a new *type* of state, a new and higher *type* of democracy, a form of the Proletarian Dictatorship, a means of administering the state *without* the bourgeoisie and *against* the bourgeoisie. For the first time democracy is here serving the people, the working people, and has ceased to be democracy for the rich as it still is in all bourgeois republics, even the most democratic. For the first time, the people are grappling, on a scale involving one hundred million, with the problem of implementing the Dictatorship of the Proletariat and Semi-Proletariat—a problem which, if not solved, makes socialism *out of the question.*

"Let the pedants, or the people whose minds are incurably stuffed with bourgeois-democratic or parliamentary prejudices, shake their heads in perplexity about our Soviets, about the absence of direct elections, for example. These people have forgotten nothing and have learned nothing during the period of the great upheavals of 1914-18. The combination of the Proletarian Dictatorship with the new democracy for the working people—of civil war with the widest participation of the people in politics—such a combination cannot be brought about at one stroke, nor does it fit in with the outworn modes of routine parliamentary democracy. The contours of a new world, the world of socialism, are rising before us in the shape of the Soviet Republic. It is not surprising that this world does not come into being ready-made, does not spring forth like Minerva from the head of Jupiter.

"The old bourgeois-democratic constitutions waxed eloquent about formal equality and right of assembly; but our proletarian and peasant Soviet Constitution casts aside the hypocrisy of formal equality. When the bourgeois republicans overturned thrones they did not worry about formal equality between monarchists and republicans. When it is a matter of overthrowing the bourgeoisie, only traitors or idiots can demand formal equality of rights for the bourgeoisie. 'Freedom of assembly' for workers and peasants is not worth a farthing when the best buildings belong to the bourgeoisie. Our Soviets have *confiscated* all the good buildings in town and country from the rich and have *transferred* all of them to the workers and peasants for *their* unions and meetings. This is our *freedom* of assembly—for the working people! This is the meaning and content of our Soviet, our socialist Constitution!

"That is why we are all so firmly convinced that no matter what misfortunes may still be in store for it, our Republic of Soviets is *invincible*."

"It is invincible because every blow struck by frenzied imperialism, every defeat the international bourgeoisie inflict on us, rouses more and more sections of the workers and peasants to the struggle, teaches them at the cost of enormous sacrifice, steels them and engenders new heroism on a mass scale.

"We know that help from you will probably not come soon, comrade American workers, for the revolution is developing in different countries in different forms and at different tempos (and it cannot be otherwise). We know that although the European proletarian revolution has been maturing very rapidly lately, it may, after all, not flare up within the next few weeks. We are banking on the inevitability of the world revolution, but this does not mean that we are such fools as to bank on the revolution inevitably coming on a *definite* and early date. We have seen two great revolutions in our country, 1905 and 1917, and we know revolutions are not made to order, or by agreement. We know that circumstances brought *our* Russian detachment of the socialist proletariat to the fore not because of our merits, but because of the exceptional backwardness of Russia, and that *before* the world revolution breaks out a number of separate revolutions may be defeated.

"In spite of this, we are firmly convinced that we are invincible, because the spirit of mankind will not be broken by the imperialist slaughter. Mankind will vanquish it. And the first country to *break* the convict chains of the imperialist war was *our* country. We sustained enormously heavy casualties in the struggle to break these chains, but we *broke* them. We are *free from* imperialist dependence, we have raised the banner of struggle for the complete overthrow of imperialism for the whole world to see.

"We are now, as it were, in a besieged fortress, waiting for the other detachments of the world socialist revolution to come to our relief. These detachments *exist*, they are *more numerous* than ours, they are maturing, growing, gaining more strength the longer the brutalities of imperialism continue. The workers are breaking away from their social traitors—the Gomperses, Hendersons, Renaudels, Scheidemanns and Renners. Slowly but surely the workers are adopting communist, Bolshevik tactics and are marching towards the proletarian revolution, which alone is capable of saving dying culture and dying mankind.

"In short, we are invincible, because the world proletarian revolution is invincible."

Vladimir Lenin

From this, it is clear that Lenin had the utmost respect for American workers. With good reason! They have previously taken part in two great revolutionary movements. The first was the "Great, really liberating, really revolutionary war", of 1776, in which the American people overthrew the British, which held them in "Colonial slavery". The second, was the "Civil War" of 1861, in which "rule of the slaveowners" was overthrown, a civil war which was both "legitimate and necessary".

This is to stress the fact, that Lenin distinguished between "wars of conquest", which are to be condemned, as opposed to revolutionary civil wars, which are necessary to overthrow the reactionary ruling class.

As this applies to our current situation, we have the American ruling class of monopoly capitalists, the multi billionaires, the bourgeoisie, which have decided to change their method of rule. The democratic republic is to be replaced with an Oligarchy, defined as "Government By the Few", otherwise known as a "Plutocracy". The extremely rich think they have the "Divine Right To Rule"!

The American democratic republic must be defended. For that reason, it is necessary to overthrow the Oligarchy. That calls for another Civil War. Just as the First Civil War was necessary, in order to overthrow the completely reactionary class of slave owners, so too, a Second Civil War is necessary, in order to overthrow the completely reactionary class of bourgeoisie, who are determined to set up an Oligarchy.

This "Second Civil War" may also be referred to as the "Second American Revolution", because that is precisely the case!

The precise name is not nearly as important, as the act of overthrowing the ruling class of bourgeoisie, of crushing the Oligarchy. That is a truly *revolutionary war!* Americans have done this before-*twice*- and they will no doubt, do it again!

In conclusion, now is the time to intensify preparations for the Insurrection, which will "kick off" the Revolution. Even though we have no way of knowing precisely when that Insurrection will take place, we do know that President Trump and "Co-President" Musk, are determined to "force the issue". It may happen sooner than we anticipate! We had best be prepared!

Just as Councils -Soviets- first appeared in Russia, as a result of the revolutionary motion, so too, Councils have also appeared in America. These Councils must be supported and strengthened, in preparation for the approaching Revolution.

Just as the Russian Soviets played a key role in the Russian Revolution, so too, the American Councils will play a key role, in the next American Revolution.

As I have gone into this in previous writings, there is no need to repeat it here. As well, I can only repeat that American attorneys, those who are experts in Constitutional law, should challenge the 2024 Presidential Election, on the grounds that it violates the Twelfth Amendment.

For the moment, in preparation for the approaching Revolution, may our signs and posters read:

Crush the Oligarchy!

Workers of the World, Unite!

Scientific Socialism!

Dictatorship of the Proletariat!